DROUGHT

DROUGHT

A NOVEL BY
SCOTT ALEXANDER HESS

REBEL SATORI PRESS
New Orleans & New York

Published in the United States of America by
Rebel Satori ImprPress
www.rebelsatoripress.com

Copyright © 2025 by Scott Alexander Hess

All rights reserved. Except for brief passages quoted in newspaper, magazine, radio, television, or online reviews, no part of this book may be reproduced in any form or any means, electronic or mechanical, including photocopying, recording, or information or retrieval system, without the permission in writing from the publisher. Please do not participate in or encourage piracy of copyrighted materials in violation of the author's rights. Purchase only authorized editions.

This is a work of fiction. Names, characters, places, and incidents are the product of the author's imagination and are used fictitiously and any resemblance to actual persons, living or dead, business establishments, events, or locales is entirely coincidental. The publisher does not have any control over and does not assume any responsibility for author or third-party websites or their content.

Cover design by Brian Alessandro

Paperback ISBN: 978-1-60864-358-5

Also By Scott Alexander Hess

*The Root of Everything and Lightning:
Two Novellas*

A Season in Delhi

PART ONE
THE FARM

CHAPTER 1

It came sudden like a fist, a rushing thing thrown from a bucket, and it startled Parnell and he struggled to sit up in the seat too small for his girth, too tight hip to hip, in the back of the Greyhound bus. Slowly and with great effort, he pulled himself up inch by inch for a clearer look through the window, taking in the onslaught of summer rain. The slanted rush of it flew steady and the blur got worse, so Parnell settled back again. He had never witnessed a storm of such violence, of such biblical reckoning, certainly not from the back of a bus in the middle of the night.

In the front pocket of his overalls, which were his lie since he was not a farmer though he now owned a farm, he found a jumbo-sized Snickers bar. It was warmish, living there in the dark against his hot skin in the warm bus. The front wrapper had printed on it: "Slice N Share" Because it was so big, he guessed.

He unwrapped it very carefully. He did not like to lose any of the chocolate to the paper, and he would not lick the paper no matter how sad and empty the bus was. No, he would not do that. He was not much, but he had manners.

The paper came off without much fuss and he began to eat. He did so with leisure and much pleasure, finishing it, licking his fingers which got stained. The sink in the Greyhound bathroom, the putrid little bathroom he could not fit in without letting the door creep open a bit, that sink did not work a lick, so he could not wash the chocolate off.

At once came a crashing roar, a sound so intense and violent it set the driver on edge up front, made him jump at the wheel, the bus careening for a moment as the bathroom door snapped open then swung shut again with a rattle while the driver corrected back into his lane. The door did not catch right, and it swung back open as the sky thundered again. *Like God bowling*, Parnell remembered they'd say at the orphanage. When a storm set its teeth in hard and knocked out a sound that felt bigger than the world itself. God's bowling. Parnell wondered if God always made a strike.

Parnell pressed his face to the bus window, peering through the drench to see the next ragged shard of light which came before the thunder. It was a nice light show during the long trip.

The bus slowed. It was turning. Parnell could not see clearly through the rain. The bathroom door snapped open again, and he thought of a scene in an old black-and-white film where it rained heavy on a farm and the barn door swung violently open and shut over and over while lightning split the sky. He loved films. They gave him comfort.

The bus came to a stop. The rain raged less. The driver spoke, cussing Parnell, though it was hard to hear him as he was up front. The electric lever that opened the door squeaked. The driver stepped out. The bus was near to empty. Several rows up, an old man snored despite the ruckus. Maybe drunk. There was a young woman following the driver out. And there was a lady with a kid.

Parnell was not sure what state they'd gotten to. Was it Virginia or had they found Kentucky? Gingerly, afraid now, rattled by the tremendous rage of that thunder, he stood up, steadied himself, then turned sideways and cautiously made his way up the narrow bus aisle. There was no longer the sound of hard rain, and the thunder had subsided. At the bus door which the driver had left open, he balanced himself and peered out.

The lit yellow sign swaying high up on a pole said *Loves Travel Stop*. Beyond that, a long squat building lit up and cheerful. It was not far to get to Love's door. The rain was a mist. Still, he wished the rain would stop all together. It could be slippery. But he needed food. It was worth the risk.

He took his time, getting out of the bus. Being so large, it was not easy. But he'd always been hefty (*fatty, lardo, beast* – those echoes) and it was part of living. Turning slightly, he stepped. If he fell, it would be very hard to get himself up, and it would take several strong men to lift him, grunting or cussing, not hiding their disgust. He needed to avoid falling. Always. He moved slow enough so as to not stumble, crossing the parking lot. He got to the door, out of breath and suddenly afraid. Looking back at the bus, the door still open, he thought: *That is then, this is the way to my new life.* He went in.

CHAPTER 2

Inside it was very bright, fluorescent bright, and he thought again: *This is cheerful.* There was a long shiny counter, a few tables and several wide red booths for groups, stretching out across the restaurant. Near the door where he stood dripping a little from the scant rain, he saw off to the left two tall circular stands selling sunglasses, hats, tote bags, odd cylinder-shaped foam rubber, and a third stand only with potato chips which looked appealing. Plus, a square wooden old-fashioned magazine rack filled with some kind of brochures.

Coming toward him at a good pace was a woman from another film he'd seen, this one from the '70s. He couldn't recall the name of the film, but this woman seemed like that woman, a sack-like upper body on long sturdy legs, a pink uniform and apron, white nylons, and a really big head of hair ratted up into a bun held with three cylinders that might be knitting needles. She spoke to him fast, and he did not at first understand, standing immobile and silent. She tried again.

"Pick yer poison," she said again more loudly as if he might be deaf.

Because of his bigness, people often assigned him other disabilities, as if it was just a natural thing. Too big, can't hear well, can't see the menu, not happy. Needs help. Trouble.

She smiled broadly. Holding up a large oblong menu shiny with grease, she swatted it toward him, which made Parnell jump; but then she turned, waving the menu in the air and indicating a big red booth. He got there at a decent pace, but as always careful. It was a very large booth. He was glad. He settled down on one side, springs under the red vinyl cushion squeaking terribly. He hoped it wouldn't sag and break.

"Ain't got real booze," she said, not seeming to notice the squeak. "Beer or coffee to start ya off?"

She gave him the menu and left, not waiting for a reply about the drink. The menu had multiple pages and was slippery to the touch. Napkins pressed out from a black plastic box. He wiped the menu front, back and each inside page.

There was only one occupied table, and he saw the back of a woman's head and her hand lifting an unlit cigarette that she drew hidden to her unseen face then brought back into view, lying her arm across the back of her booth. He did not see the bus driver.

The waitress returned. One of the knitting needles in her hair was gone. Behind her and behind the counter a big black-and-white clock read "3."

"Ya believe in prophecy?" she said. "Not me. But I might a have just then. Never heard thunder like that. And I been around."

She cawed with laughter. There were a series of windows on one wall looking out at the parking lot, the night, the stranded bus.

"Well," she said holding the note of that word, like it would keep going on.

"The Lumberjack please," Parnell said.

He had eaten at a lot of diners. He liked them. Nobody cared much about anybody else.

She did not write anything down, but rattled fast questions which he answered about breakfast meat, bread, blueberry syrup or maple, and what to drink.

He looked out again toward the bus. It sat dark. The rain was coming and going but was softer. The bus driver strode past him. He stopped at the booth where the lady whose back faced him was sitting with her unlit cigarette. The bus driver nodded, smiled, seemed to be making nice. Then he sat across from her.

Parnell did not wonder why he didn't sit with him. People were not as a rule fond of him. Especially strangers. He knew he was an odd sight to most. Tall and wide like a truck. Six foot, 310 pounds. A big head and big feet. He was glad he had an eye on the bus driver. He did not want to be left behind.

The waitress was back with a platter of food, his Lumberjack. He wondered if it was cooked earlier, set aside like forgotten things, a dead woman's china, a useless toy rattle. It seemed to have come out so quickly.

She set the large plate in front of him, then sat across from him. He did not like people to watch him eat, and he had never seen a waitress sit so unexpectedly with a customer. He glanced out the window, not knowing what else to do, how to rid himself of her, but out there was the dark bus and the night without any rain now, without any color.

"Hope you don't mind, but I just need a sit," she said. "And that old boy, back by the bathroom booth, is grabby. You know.

Just let me stop here if you don't mind."

She said it with desperation, like a confession, and he understood. He knew those feelings. She was not acting the way she looked, harsh and funny. She was acting like a lost thing. She turned her face and he saw a spot on her cheek where makeup had been piled heavy, like caulking to cover a hole where a picture nail had damaged the wall. He took up a piece of bacon and ate it. She kept her face turned out that way, which gave Parnell courage.

"You have a beauty mark" he said. "Why did you cover it up?"

She did not turn, just put one hand on the spot. As if they were good friends, as if they were having a whiskey at a bar and talking about old times. She brought her hand to her face with a sense of "Oh my," with a touch of whimsy. But it was not that.

"It ain't becoming," she said with finality.

Then she stood up abruptly. She smiled and the fleeting look of loss was drawn back in somewhere past that frayed pink apron, somewhere in her gut where she kept things hid so she could survive. He understood that too.

"Where ya headed, Friend?" she said smiling. "Everybody's on their way somewhere when they stop at Love's."

Parnell paused in his eating and drew a folded-up map out of the front of his overalls, a large pocket there.

"Frattsville, Kentucky," he said. "Do you know it?"

She touched her cheek, and he wondered if she might rub off the makeup, reveal the mark that was under, tell him something real. But she did not.

"You mean Fredsville. That's what you mean. Another four

hours west."

Considering the food, which was his main concern, Parnell wrestled with what to do, but decided it was best to set the woman straight. He did not tolerate being told he was wrong. He put up with a lot, but he did not let people intentionally indicate that he was stupid. He pulled another piece of paper from the front pocket of his overalls.

"It's Frattsville," he said, unfolding and holding up what was a deed for a farm. "This proves it. This is mine."

A man began singing from the back of the restaurant. Parnell imagined it was the grabby man. She leaned in, looking closely.

"Well, look at that," she said softly, almost with respect. "Sure is. I guess I been wrong a long time. Are you a farmer?"

The bus driver was rising. He was moving toward them. He did not acknowledge Parnell, and Parnell knew in his gut the man did not care for him and would saunter out the door to the bus, snap shut the door, and drive away without a look back.

Parnell quickly folded some of the food into a napkin as he thought how to answer the waitress. He thought hard about who he was going to become, since where he came from had no hold on him, and there was no sense of anything at all he had to cling to or remain devoted to. In short, his life was dull, empty, and had up to now been directionless.

The chalk was poised in his big hand, and he saw it move, and he thought, *I won't look back anymore and I have a right to do this.*

"I'm going to farm tobacco."

He piled more food into folded napkins and followed the

waitress to where they ran the checks, moving as fast as his girth would allow; then he made it out to the bus just as the bus driver was shutting the door.

CHAPTER 3

The rain was done, all traces dried to dust, and Parnell thought, *I never guessed the sun could be this hot.*

It was morning. He was standing on his land, yes, *his* because the deed said so, because the lawyer had explained and because he believed (as there was no other logical reason) that it was because of an act of kindness from a man he did not know. Parnell had never written to his one relative, his Uncle Willy. When he was eight, the institutional housing where he lived had revealed this found Uncle. Had asked him if he would like to write to him. "We told him about you," a spindly prune-faced woman had said. "Do you want to write and ask him to visit." "No," Parnell said. He knew he was an oddity. Obese, they said. Nobody would willingly want him. Even so young, he felt it was not right to force things. Still, the idea of him must have left an imprint on Old Willy. Because he'd left Parnell the farm.

Standing in the yard, there was a rising cry, which Parnell knew were locusts because he had seen a film where the insects screeched loudly and often and then someone died terribly in a car wreck. He could not recall the name of the film. He could rarely remember the names of the films, any films, but images of those films smoldered in his brain like memories. Memories he lay claim to.

His actual memories, the low-grade remembering's of things that had gone on unceremoniously, uneventfully and often in ugly ways, paled and fell to shadow against the films' rememberings. He had nothing worth holding onto in his own lived life. The films would do just fine.

He felt heat growing right up from the ground where he stood, pushing forcibly up his legs, all over his body, making him sweat, and he thought again, *I did not know it could be so hot all at once and after so much rain.*

There was the sound of a car approaching. He turned away from the land, which stretched very far out. Coming up a gravel road that spit out from the two-lane was a blue Buick. It stopped in the front of the small frail house which was also now his.

Stepping out of the car was a tall lean man with very long legs. Insect legs, Parnell thought, like a creature born of the too loud locusts. The man moved toward him and Parnell wondered if he should be afraid; but as the man came closer, he spoke in a loud, artificially friendly voice which Parnell recognized.

"We spoke on the phone. I'm Diggs. Mr. Diggs. Just came to see if you got in all right."

He was the lawyer, who had called and surprised him with the whole thing. His uncle's will, the farm being his.

"I didn't think you'd come," Mr. Diggs said, striding closer on those too long legs, in a blue suit that puckered oddly around the waist and shoulders and seemed an odd choice in the heat. "I came to see."

He stood next to Parnell, his radical leanness in sharp

contrast to the expanse of Parnell. They both looked out at the land. There came then, from a distance, a hard and unearthly sound, like a dozen strings of music pushing against each other in some terrible fight. It was floating on the air. It rose then fell.

Mr. Diggs put his hands in his pockets.

"There she is," he said.

The sound had risen a bit more, then stopped abruptly.

"What?" Parnell said.

The man, a stranger really, turned quickly, pulled his hands free of his pockets, and brought back that loud, artificial voice he'd started with when he'd first shouted from the car.

"Sunday. The church is a few miles, but it carries. The old pipes."

"I don't understand." Parnell said.

"He's a local guy. Darl. He hits it a little hard, but at least there's music at church."

He smiled broadly.

"Don't worry, only on Sundays. Maybe Friday for practice. But then that's what I was telling you on the phone. It's a big deal, getting all this. But now that you're here. Have you thought of what I said?"

Parnell did not like the man. He was barely off the bus, barely recognizing the magnitude of his great fortune, the sheer shape and opportunity of it all. He did not want to recall what the man had said, did not care and did not want to consider what he'd relegated to shadow thought. He kept his eyes looking out. He did not say a word. There was a quiver of sound, as if the organ would begin, but it died out.

"Like I told you, there's a buyer. I can sew it up so you don't have to do anything but sign a few papers and take the check."

Parnell remained still, waiting for the man to leave. Mr. Diggs began to lift his hand to shake, but dropped it and turned back to his car. He stopped, his back to Parnell, and said in a voice he had not yet used at all, a darker very clear voice,

"Farming is not something you can just show up and do. It's not like opening a can of coffee."

There was a pause.

"And they say a drought's coming."

Parnell did not turn. He heard the feet across gravel, the engine rev up, the car back out and drive off. He stood alone in the heat on his land, hoping the organ might begin to play again. But it did not.

CHAPTER 4

Parnell slept through the day.

He had slept solidly, despite the heat and lying in a curtainless room on a lumpy bed not large enough for him (no bed ever was). He woke at dusk. He did not have that odd moment of fear, waking in a new place, the dream-mind torn in half and thinking, *Where is this?* He woke as if he'd been there a long time, as if he knew the place. He took his time getting up.

Old Uncle Willy had left the house in good shape. Clean, simple, well put together. It was two stories. Just past the front door, a worn cedar staircase shot straight up to a second floor bedroom and bath. The bed (only a full) had been made, a quilt of blue diamonds laid out. There was a fan. The electric was left on.

Downstairs was also whistle clean and simple. A main room with a fireplace, near a small dining room with a hutch, and then a large kitchen with a table. Plus another bathroom and a bedroom with a king-sized bed which was fine and meant he did not need to haul himself up to the second floor one step at a time to a bed too small anyway.

In the kitchen, Parnell sensed the old man's presence like a lingering breath, and he believed Uncle Willy expected him to stay and make a go of it. The place had been rightly prepared for him, he felt.

At the kitchen table, made of the same cedar used on the stairs, Parnell sat studying a book he'd brought on tobacco farming.

The average tobacco farm in Kentucky consists of 113 acres, with 4.6 acres being the average tobacco acreage planted. Farming the crop is labor intensive. Many tobacco farming families in this region have children who continue to miss classes and eventually drop out of school.

Parnell paused, considering the last few words about the kids. The book was current. He did not want to get discouraged, but he felt as if he'd been dropped into another time, or onto one of his shadow memory film sets, where children quit school to farm. He shut the large book.

The lawyer was right, he knew nothing about farming. Still, he already dismissed his old life, that unremarkable and drab routine. There was nothing to run back to, no one expecting him, and he had already set in motion what would be his future. There was only this.

Over the sink was a window which he'd opened in the heat, and through that came a momentarily strong breeze. It smelled of rain, or something damp and dark, and it blew straight at him then ceased. Parnell believed in most anything, since there was no harm in it, so he decided the breeze was some last breath of Uncle Willy, a strong urging to trust what had been given so freely. There was also a truck. The keys to the truck sat on the table across from him, and he half expected a new breeze to push them clear across the table into his hand.

It was dark, he was in back country, but he was also hungry

and had nothing in the house to eat. He would get on the road, and he would find the town.

CHAPTER 5

Behind the house was a barn. It was ancient looking, with a peaked roof, walls of battered wood showing shades of red, faded yellow and dull brown, like every piece had seen all sorts of rough weather. Two wide-plank doors in front were partially open. The bottom lip of the right-side door was stuck so deep in mud Parnell wondered if it had been like that for years, if old Uncle Willy liked it that way. It looked desperate, like it might never move forward or back, might never feel complete and safe in its full closing position again. Parnell felt bad for the door since a door was meant to both open and shut. Everything had a purpose.

He struggled slowly through the high grass behind the house, sweat rolling in thin rivulets across his entire body, this wetness now a part of what was going to be his plight in this place. It was a new slickness that he didn't bother to try to halt. He was a big person and big people sweat. The heat was constant, and there was a new humidity the rain had left behind. Like an afterthought, a warning.

Parnell hoped the locals wouldn't mock him for the patches of sweat on his shirt, under his armpits, around his collar, matting his dark hair. But he had dealt with discomfort and sneers his entire life. It was one of the few things he understood.

And he was deeply proud of his ability to withstand discomfort.

The stuck door was not quite open wide enough for Parnell to easily get through. Or the truck for that matter. He could see into the dark barn, and the white of the pick-up truck glowed like a glossed tooth. Something cawed loudly from a patch of woods west of the house, and Parnell gasped. He was going to have to get used to sounds like that, things he did not know, could not imagine. He took a deep breath, put both hands on the edge of the door and pushed. His weight came in handy at times. His bulk, in the right position, could be put to use. He'd once used his shoulder to push a very large refrigerator across an entire room. The door scraped in the mud, squeaked and pleaded not to be dislodged from its long-stuck home. But slowly and with effort, Parnell succeeded and the door moved a few feet.

He stepped in.

It was even hotter in the barn. He saw no windows, no cracks in the walls that moonlight might pass through. It was like a tomb. But the truck shone brightly.

His eyes were adjusted fully to the night, and he made out a few neat piles of hay, a pitchfork and a big dead-looking tractor in a far back corner. He knew the set-up from so many films, some dark and forgotten because a terrible figure did a terrible thing to a teenager, but more clearly he recalled the black-and-white moment where the girl sat on the bale and sang, and he cried (not just the first time alone watching, but every time), and he felt as if she stepped closer to him, the watcher, touched his hot cheek and kissed him. This was a memory not just soft in shadow but fully formed and retrievable. It was real and he knew he would never lose it. It was part of him.

The truck's car door window was rolled all the way down. He pulled the door open, then heaved himself up slowly and in two large grunting pulls, using the car door and the side. He was breathing heavy by the time he got up into the truck. It was the type of truck with one long seat from side to side and a cargo bed in back.

He could not adjust the seat back any further, so driving would be awkward. There was barely enough room. He pressed back into the seat to get his arms around the wheel and turn it side to side, making sure it could move despite the closeness to his belly. It was not impossible, to drive this, but he would need to be very careful.

It was a stick shift. There was no radio but an ashtray in the center which was open. There was a single cigarette butt, half smoked. He took up the butt. He paused, then put it in his mouth, guessing it was the last thing Uncle Willy had touched. The contact with his lips, that ancient flavor, shattered him for a second because the thought of the girl on the hay bale singing, her kiss had not disappeared completely, and too he imagined a dangling cigarette from Uncle Willy's mouth, and it struck him definitively that the man was dead, gone forever. He would not be back. Not for even a moment. Only his unexpected kindness to Parnell remained, which moved him greatly and also steeled his determination to make it all work, whatever it all turned out to be. It was not like someone had loved him, but someone had thought of him and that was enough.

He took the keys from the pocket in the front of his overalls. The engine turned over nicely. He left the half butt between his lips. Like chewing a toothpick. It might bring him luck.

He found the lights and turned them on bright. He put his big fist over the black bulb of the stick shift, disappearing it, and went into reverse. He did not bother to try to turn or look in the rearview mirror because he could not move that way. He backed up. The truck was in line with the open door, so as long as he remained straight, he'd get it out.

He hit the gas a bit too hard and it bolted out like a trapped horse. He hit the break. He was out of the barn. He backed up further, then turned the wheel with a good amount of difficulty to get him onto the road that led down to the two-lane.

The entry to the two-lane was very dark. He did not pause, just kept the truck moving, turning right, toward the remembered sound of the church organ and toward the town. He did not look around much, rather kept his eyes keenly on the road ahead defined by the bright circles of artificial light.

He drove steady, chewing on the cigarette butt, hearing the locusts.

There were no other cars on the road. He wondered if Uncle Willy drove fast or slow, smoked while he drove, sang out loud, drank whiskey. He wondered if there was a picture of the old man in the house. If so, he would hang it up.

Then he saw, in the distance, not far off the road, the church. It was on a patch of earth that had been cleared. There was a small dirt area for cars. The church was lit up and the warm glow of it in the utter darkness of the night was quite brilliant to see. He wondered who was in the church at night. But he dared not stop. He was not foolhardy.

Other than it being lit, it was an unremarkable church.

Parnell slowed as he came toward it. It was small and square with a steeple roof. It looked cheaply put together and a little sad. He did not turn to look back because he could not turn.

After a bit, there was another light, something bright, though he had not come to the center of town yet. It was a large sign looming on an otherwise dark and bleak landscape. It was yellow and red and black and he knew it, he knew it well and smiled and laughed out loud. It was a Sonic drive in, and in large black letters on the white board below the immense and lit sign it said: "Welcome Back. Garlic Butter Bacon Burger."

He pulled in and stopped, happy he did not have to get out of the car. He could stay put and he could get his dinner. He was very hungry. Next to the truck was the large white menu board. It was an old-school Sonic, where someone came out to take the order. He did not have to shout into a speaker.

There was only one other car in the lot. It was a very old gray Cadillac, and there was a shadowy figure slumped in the darkened front seat, and Parnell could not tell if that person was a man or woman or awake or asleep, but he was very hungry and couldn't bother with that.

He surveyed the menu. He had to decide on which Sonic Blast to order. It was his favorite part of the meal. The super thick milkshake could be made with Butterfingers, Reese's Peanut Butter Cups, cookie dough or Snickers bars. This was the hardest choice because he loved them all. He decided on Snickers since it had the most ingredients, with chocolate, caramel and nuts. He would also go with the bacon double cheeseburger combo with fries.

He waited, chewing the cigarette butt. He thought someone

would come to take his order curbside. He was getting impatient. He glanced again at the other car, wondering if there was anyone in it at all. Could anyone be that motionless, that unimportant, so as to fade into a car's interior?

There was a squealing noise, and he watched the Cadillac in its stillness, expecting to see someone rise up; then he turned, realizing the front door to the Sonic had swung open. That was the screech.

A reedy red-headed young man stood at the door watching Parnell. He wore a black-and-white checkered shirt and dungarees. He waved, which Parnell found very peculiar. Parnell thought perhaps something was terribly wrong, that the young man was motioning for him to get away before it was too late. The young man was still watching him, and Parnell started the truck back up which set the fellow in motion. He came directly to the side of Parnell's car.

"People don't want to pay the tip no more," he said, revealing a small pad and pencil. "Our car- side speakers broke last year. But most folks come in and take out. You know. Cheap."

The man looked about thirty, older than he first appeared from a distance. His face was covered with a starscape of freckles of varied sizes and shapes. It seemed nearly like an affliction, so many freckles. He wet the tip of his pencil then smiled, and Parnell realized he was putting on a show.

"What can I bring ya?" he said, smiling.

Parnell recited his order. Before the man turned to go Parnell asked:

"Is there someone in that other car?"

Without a beat, the man replied.

"That's Joe. Don't worry, he ain't dead. He farms early and when he eats a good amount here, he just falls asleep awhile. He'll be all right."

The young man leaned a little closer, surveying the inside of the truck.

"You farm? Never seen you here?"

"I have a tobacco farm," Parnell said with pride, with joy because the words came out with a certain effortlessness and confidence that he was not at all used to in his life.

"Is that right?"

"It was my Uncle Willy's farm. It's mine now."

"Oh sure, Willy sure. Good guy. I'll be back with your food in a jiffy."

With that the man turned away, but as he left he yelled, "I'm Darl."

Parnell smiled. He wasn't used to friendly people, especially not when he was ordering food. There was very little warmth or humanity in spots like this. He felt welcome.

There was a rumble and headlights lit. It was the Cadillac. Parnell could see the man in the car now, turning to look behind him as he backed out. He noticed Parnell and waved, and Parnell waved back. It was turning into quite a night.

6

Darl came back out with the food on a cheap silver tray.

"Roll the window up a bit," Darl said.

With great effort, Parnell turned at the waist so his wide right arm could reach the window crank. Darl watched the effort.

"It needs to hang there," Darl said, carefully positioning the tray with its two long silver mounting arms on the window. "Nobody and I mean nobody does this anymore anywhere. We keep it alive. The window hang."

Darl winked. It was like he was in an old TV ad.

Parnell was waiting for him to leave. He did not like being watched while he ate. Darl looked up at the night sky.

"Not a soul inside. I gotta admit I was happy when you pulled up. It's a long night here. An awfully long night."

He looked down and smiled, then he glanced back at the restaurant.

"Guess I'll stock some straws. That's what I'll do," he said smiling. "I'll be back to get the tray."

He turned to go but the slow way he moved, as if he really wanted to turn back, to linger, touched Parnell.

"I'm Parnell." He said from the truck.

Darl turned quickly. Bowing, then tipping his cheap white

paper hat.

"Good meeting you, Parnell."

Parnell watched him disappear back into the Sonic. He felt in his gut that he had somehow made things a little easier for this strange man, that he – Parnell – had done something useful.

7

Parnell, as a rule, did not like films where young people became lost on a rural road. He didn't like them because of the film with the blue car and the troop of college students near Appalachia. It was a film from 1980 that set his teeth on edge, that left a hard imprint on his mind that he could not erase. Not just the carnage, but even the shade of the car's blue, a shimmering and bright blue, disturbed him because it was too beautiful a vehicle to be in such a depraved motion picture.

Driving down the empty two-lane, his comfort from the food began to seep away as the unwanted memory of the blue car took shape. He was frightened and that was not good while he was driving on this unknown road in this pitch-black night.

Luckily, the light came. First, a glimmer in the distance, like someone's dying campfire, but then very quickly it was a solid thing, a bold thing in the emptiness.

It was the church he had passed on his way to the Sonic. It was lit from within.

He drove, creeping closer and closer, then pulled off the road and into the gravel lot fronting the church. He needed to feel safe. And churches were safe. Even in frightening films. They were safe.

He stopped and shut off the truck. The locusts screeched

loudly. There were other night sounds he did not know. But from the church came no sound, only the light which in its brightness calmed him.

He wrenched opened the truck door, the mechanical and unnatural squeak of it ugly against the song of the locust. He slowly wrangled himself out of the cramped vehicle.

As he began to walk toward a pair of high wooden doors, he wondered why they left the place lit up. It seemed like a waste, maybe even a sin.

At the door, there was a gentle noise. He leaned and listened. Someone was praying. Parnell was in a tortured moment, not wanting to disturb the devotee but needing to get into the light, to dispel the hard little memory of the wicked blue car in Appalachia.

Poised there, he felt the night's darkness closing in on him, bringing with it a too vivid memory of a scraggly-haired hillbilly with a scar and an eyepatch and an ax. He stepped in quietly.

The church was austere and simple. Ten stiff-looking wooden pews on each side, an altar and an organ. He hoped the man praying up front did not hear him. He felt terrible, like a thief stealing solace. The man, who sat in the front pew, was speaking out loud, and soon Parnell could make out words, phrases, the way he'd made out the dissonant melody of the church's organ from a distance.

"For which of you, intending to build a tower, does not first sit down and estimate the cost, to see whether he has enough to complete it? Otherwise…"

He paused, then spoke in a much louder voice.

"When he has laid a foundation and is not able to finish, all who see it will begin to ridicule him, saying…"

The man stood up wearily. He was small, wiry and young-looking from Parnell's vantage point. He ran his hands through his hair, which was black and wild like a tangle of snakes.

"No, Saint Luke," he said. "That's gonna fall flat as a pancake and I can't make that sing."

At once, he grabbed the scraggle of hair on the top of his head, tilted back and began to moan. It was edged and ripe with anger and, Parnell thought, full of loss.

Parnell stepped forward. He did not like being spied on and he would not do it to this man.

"Are you all right?" Parnell said, trying to sound concerned.

The man spun on him.

"Of course I'm all right."

In a black-collared short-sleeved shirt and dark pants, he appeared very fit, sinewy with veins popping on his naked forearms. But his face was ravaged, wrecked by something. He looked beaten down.

"I'm sorry," Parnell said, turning.

"No! Good Lord, no! God's house is not for me, but for you, friend," he said. "Please join me. I'm just wrestling with a gospel is all. I lost track."

The man sounded saner now, and the light felt gentle again, the pews comforting, so he walked toward him.

"Are you the preacher?" he asked.

"Yes, I am. Yes, yes, that's right."

"And this is your church?"

The man's face fell. It literally fell, like it had been done in clay and had been blasted with heat and was melting downward.

He spoke softly, sadly.

"It is ours, son," the man said. "But they see it as mine. That's my problem."

He turned away, and Parnell felt as if he had ruined the man, as if he were the last push that led him to give up on something he'd been doing for a long, long time.

"Sit with me, son," the man said wearily.

Then, with his back to Parnell, he waved him on and sat in the front pew.

"I am the pastor here. See, I should have said that right away, don't you think?"

Parnell stood by the pew. He gave it a good look. He had to be certain it could hold him. He had split a few cheaply made benches in his lifetime. He leaned on it casually. It was solid. He sat with a thud.

"I'm sorry to disturb you," Parnell said.

The preacher turned to him, smiling.

"That thought should not come to mind. You should think..."

He looked forward, at a rather rudimentary though large depiction of Christ on the cross which hung behind the small altar. Jesus had been carved of wood and hung on wood. But the wood was all the same shade, so his body faded into the cross like it was all one thing. It had little impact.

They sat quietly, save for the sounds of the locusts. Then the sound of a car passing, drifting toward them, becoming louder then, sweeping away with the life in the vehicle fading.

"Will you come to church Sunday?" the preacher said.

"Yes," Parnell said.

He wasn't sure how the man knew who he was, or where he was from, but he seemed so desperate Parnell immediately agreed. And he knew he would show up. If for nothing else, because he was a man of his word. He also wanted to hear the organ up close.

"I've heard the organ," Parnell said.

The preacher sat up.

"Yes, by God, yes. Darl is getting pretty good."

"From the Sonic?"

"Yes, are you friends?"

"Yes," Parnell said boldly, without a beat.

He stood up and said his thanks, his goodbyes, because the fear had evaporated, and he was ready to go home. As he got into his truck, he thought, *Darl is my friend.* That felt true. And that truth lit him up.

8

The sun blazed high above the Sonic. It was a bold, strong sun, and it was already a very hot day. There was not a cloud in the sky, which was a watery white blue as if the sun's heat had burnt the color away.

Parnell was enjoying a SuperSonic breakfast burrito. He'd woken very early, to a house empty of any provisions. He'd set out for the local grocery store, but his hunger overwhelmed him on the way to town. He stopped at the Sonic hoping to see Darl.

Instead, a buxom blonde woman wearing short shorts and a checkerboard top had waited on him.

The girl, now bringing the French toast sticks he'd decided to add to his burrito order, did not look at him as she dropped off the food. She turned away, as if another customer needed her. There was no one else at the place.

She reminded him of so many people he had encountered through his life, people who did not hide their disgust. They would see him, then quickly look away. As if just seeing him could infect them.

An engine roared. A souped-up red Mustang pulled in next to his truck. Smiling through the open window was Darl.

"Wait a minute!" Darl said loudly, bounding out of the car. "You moving in here?"

He was at the side of Parnell's truck, at the window, and Parnell felt happy.

"I guess I can say the same thing," Parnell said.

He was not a witty man, he did not say witty things, but the moment had presented itself and there was something about Darl's openness that gave Parnell a foreign courage. He knew it was all part of the change that was happening, a psychic change that had been tricked into motion the moment Uncle Willy died. He was sure of that. The rude buxom woman could not reverse that. No one could.

Darl laughed out loud.

"The old guy brings the paychecks this morning, but you got a point. I ought to be in bed, not at this joint. But in this heat, who can sleep? They say buckle up. Drought is here to stay. And a stretch of 100-degree days brother!"

The young woman leaned out the door and waved.

"Hey, Bea," Darl said.

"He's late," she barked, disappearing back inside.

"You got Old Willy's place," Darl said, for a moment leaning onto Parnell's truck hood but yanking back fast because the metal was hot to the touch. "Word gets around. Everybody knows everything here."

The blonde was back, shouting.

"Two hours," she said.

Darl turned and looked up at the sun, folding his arms.

"Damn it," he said, still staring up at that broad hot sun. "What the hell. I ain't going all the way back home."

Parnell had several French toast sticks in his right hand, which was inside the truck dangling at his side. He let them drop to the floor, not wanting to eat them with Darl looking on. Parnell paused, then looked up at the same sun Darl was fixed on and said simply,

"Would you like to come see my farm?"

Darl laughed out loud again.

"Well hell, yes sir! Old Willy never asked me out there that's for sure. Let's go!"

Darl moved at a furious clip toward his bright red Mustang, yanked open the door and swung in, and Parnell sighed quietly at the sight, having never had the capacity to move or swing into anything with such grace.

The Mustang's motor revved dangerously. Darl shouted something and spun the car back onto the road and Parnell followed.

9

The barn was bigger in daylight. The bold Kentucky sun burnt straight through a threading series of veins in the structure's walls, creating line after line of intense light. It was heavenly, Parnell thought, not at all ghostly as he'd imagined that first night he witnessed the hay bales, the truck, the pitchfork. He began to recall a happy barn film about a horse and a boy, but the sound of Darl rough-kicking the side of the tractor, then whistling long and loud drew him back.

"She's old, but a beauty," Darl said, climbing onto the tractor's rusted metal seat. "You'd think she was dead, but no sir. She's got life."

Parnell moved closer to the machine. The actual physical beast of the tractor brought on the mysterious reality of farming. He had no idea what he was doing and he could not imagine himself on the tractor if for no other reason than he was way too broad to fit in the small seat. Plus, everything had a weight limit (he once had to step out of a crowded elevator at the request of a tiny nervous woman). Did they make extra-large tractor seats? He imagined all farmers to be large people. Hearty. But looking at Darl, who was smiling broadly and still whistling, he realized it might not be the case.

"I can bring her back to life," Darl said.

He stayed on the tractor, as if he owned it, and Parnell wondered if his new friend might flip a switch and get the thing to rev up and speed out into the field like he did with his Mustang. Instead, he gave Parnell a good long stare.

"Can I tell you something?" Darl said.

"Sure," Parnell said.

Parnell wished he could sit, or lean against a pole, or do something he'd seen cowboys do in films that made them look comfortable and strong and ready to hear a story. Instead, he simply stood still and waited, sweating profusely in the hot barn. He knew not to try to sit, certainly not on a box or the ground. Sitting was a strenuous operation and getting back up was even tougher.

"I really wanted to see this place," Darl said. "Your uncle. He kept to himself. I can't say I know anyone that's stepped foot onto this farm for, heck, ten years or more. Except the preacher. Yeah, he's been here."

He looked at Parnell as if it was his turn to reveal something, or to be the storyteller. But Parnell knew nothing about Uncle Willy. He had hoped the locals would reveal things. In the awkward pause, he felt ashamed. How does one not know their own family? How can one accept an inheritance from a man he barely knew?

"Aw, just tell me to shut my trap and mind my business," Darl said, gripping the tractor's steering wheel and turning it back and forth like a boy playing. "Ask anybody, I'm always asking questions I shouldn't. Got knocked on my ass in a bar a few times for just thinking I was being conversational. Anyway, I'm glad to help out. What's the plan?"

With this, Parnell saw an opening.

"I don't have a plan," he said. "I don't really know anything about farming."

There was a brief frozen pause, then Darl cut loose with an extremely loud rambunctious laugh. His thin body shook, and his freckled face turned bright red; then, rocking with laughter, he fell out of the seat and landed on the hard ground. Still, he continued to laugh, there on the ground, before catching his breath.

Getting up to a kneeling position brought Darl's full figure into a vein of light which gave him a cinematic look, a look Parnell knew so well from countless Westerns.

"You are a certified hoot. Who in the hell takes on a farm like this not knowing his ass from a tobacco leaf?"

Parnell stepped back, fearing the man may stand up, come at him, knock him over, call him stupid. Instead, Darl stood, brushed dirt off his ass and smiled.

"That's a whole bucket of courage, man," he said. "I wish I had your guts."

To Parnell, the light coming through the wood cracks brightened their scene even more, making it nearly joyous.

10

Darl, Parnell and Joe stood in the center of the farm's back acreage. It was early evening, and the flat ruined fields took on a gentle appearance, like a darkening river. Joe was the farmer Parnell had glimpsed eating at the Sonic. He was a friend of Darl's, and an expert at tobacco farming.

Joe was a sturdy man with a round, craggy face, dressed in overalls and wearing a ball cap that appeared puny on his large head. The cap cast a shadow on his face that belied measure of age. He moved with a slow but youthful grace. But his voice was ragged, as if the damaging heat and stern winds had over the years gotten into his lungs, causing a rattle that wouldn't clear up. It was a wise voice, Parnell decided.

"She's a good piece o' land," Joe said slowly, moving one arm from east to west.

At that, a horse appeared from the east, moving slowly, then at a gallop across the horizon. Then the animal stopped.

"You got a good 50 acres," Joe said. "I been cross it few times with Willy. Before he took to hisself."

He did not look at Parnell. He continued, stepping out into the acres, toward the horse which was watching them from the far distance. It shook its mane. It's smiling, Parnell thought, as it bared its teeth.

"Most here you got is useable land, ya see?" Joe said. "Just a crick due mile west, but other than that you're good. Ain't been farmed in a while. Far as I know. Which is a problem."

At this, he stopped and turned to Parnell. He smiled, baring his teeth like the horse, and Parnell felt he was meant to say something, to add a bit of knowledge about what Uncle Willy's intentions had been, leaving him the farm. Of course, he knew nothing, so he awkwardly smiled, though he did not show his teeth as they were not something to be seen. Two missing on one side and yellow.

"Can we farm this?" Parnell finally said.

Joe shrugged and turned back to the acres, still watching the horse.

"Up to you. I'm guessing you ain't a farmer by trade," Joe said. "So there's that to consider."

He waited, but Parnell remained silent.

"Tobacco can be tricky," Joe said. "Myself, I do soybeans. Too bad your uncle didn't keep things up."

There was a long pause as they stood looking out.

"Well, I'm hungry as shit," Darl said. "You got anything to eat up at that house? I never had dinner."

Joe turned and began to walk back. The watching horse shook its head and galloped back the direction it came. Parnell followed Joe, trailed by Darl.

"I don't," Parnell said,

"Say we go to Sonic. I can get us free food. What ya say, Joe?"

With his back to them, Joe still walking lifted his arm, indicating he was in.

11

From inside, washed in morning light, the timber-built church felt welcoming, which Parnell had not experienced during his first visit there a few weeks back.

Two dozen people were scattered in the hard-hewn pews. It was Sunday. Parnell was alone in the front row. He did not want to see or be distracted by anyone ahead of him, other than Jesus on the cross and the white light coming through the one window behind the altar. He feared more being stared at by living people than by Jesus.

Darl coughed. He was at the organ to Parnell's right. The cough seemed to be a signal as the preacher, wearing a traditional priest's garb of black pants and shirt with white collar, stepped from a doorway behind the organ. He did not look well. Two wide swaths of underarm sweat stained his shirt. There was a patch covering one knee of the pants. His black hair was wild and untamed, and his face was flushed. He looked like he'd run up a steep hill to get to the church on time.

Darl coughed again. The preacher moved slowly, bowed head, toward the center of the altar. One loud low note rang out from the organ. It was clearly a mistake, as Darl guffawed visibly and looked into his lap, muttering. At the altar, the preacher was motionless, head still down, in front of the small crowd of parishioners. Time crept, then finally, "Praise the Lord!"

The sound was startling. The preacher's voice was not just loud and ragged, it was a plea filled with torment and grit.

Darl cleared his throat and began to play. The music was as urgent and overwhelming as the preacher's shout. The organ wheezed and the music felt carnivalesque, not holy. Parnell did not know what the tune was, but it did not suit a church service. There were far too many erratic high notes, then off-tune dips.

Taking a deep breath and fighting an urge to flee, Parnell focused on the calming view of the light behind the altar. He'd been to very few churches, heard very few organs. He only came today to see Darl and because he'd promised the preacher.

Eyes shut, he thought of an organ in a film with Vincent Price. As the memory surfaced, he remembered it as ghastly. A threatening, mean organ that rose from the floor. Violent deaths. He opened his eyes and turned to watch Darl again.

Darl's head was bent. His arms and hands moved cross, over, up, down with fervor. There was more rising in the music, a reaching higher, it felt to Parnell, a reckoning. Then abruptly it stopped.

He was grateful for that. There were light sounds, parishioners shifting in their seats. The preacher gazed out with a dreadful look in his eyes as if he were witnessing horror.

"I looked right there in Jesus' eyes, right there in a blue fire, and I saw in his great peace my sin, my fire, because we can't escape it. It was a flame shooting out at me and it was thirsty; it wanted me and I had to turn away."

He paused and Parnell thought the man may begin to weep.

"Is our sin a fire or a drought?" he said. "Is it gnarled and weedy? Does it thirst?"

Parnell was sweating a lot. He wondered if the crowd was meant to answer or just nod. He wished he'd sat in the back so he could leave without notice.

The preacher's shoulders lowered, and he looked like he might sit on the floor. He sighed with exhaustion then, taking a deep breath, he cried out, ragged again, speaking rapidly.

"A drought is here. We all know that. So bring on the tears of Jesus. Save our land."

With effort, Parnell shifted his weight slightly to glimpse the people behind him. The small crowd was either enraptured or afraid. He couldn't be sure. He presumed they all knew the preacher, that they all had come before.

As he turned back, the preacher was holding a tin bucket and a silver wand. He dipped the wand, lifted it high, and shook out water toward the crowd. A few drops hit Parnell. The water was cooling. The preacher moved slowly out into the crowd, dipping and shaking a gentle rain.

"Do you reaffirm your renunciation of evil and renew your commitment to Jesus Christ?"

He stepped past Parnell toward the parishioners.

The rest was said quickly, loudly interrupted only by the sound of the wand knocking the tin bucket as he dipped and cast.

"Will you persevere in resisting evil? Will you seek and serve Jesus? Will you strive for the peace respect and dignity of every human being? Will you?"

There was a lull. The sound of footsteps, the setting down of the tin bucket, the preacher going to the altar, opening a large book, lifting his arms. Then he began to read in a slow and even voice, from scripture.

"Let us pray."

12

Parnell stood outside the church. It looked stark and lonely against the backdrop of the hot summer morning. The parishioners shuffled out. He was waiting for Darl. At last, Darl emerged, waved and came to where Parnell stood.

"Well, that wasn't too good. I hit a lot of bad notes."

Parnell wanted to say something nice despite his feeling that Darl was not very good. But he had no reference point for lying with purpose. He felt an urgency to speak.

"How did you learn to play?"

They stood together on the now empty lot in the sweltering heat. Parnell thought, "I should have just said let's go eat. Or you did a great job." His doubt flamed high. He was not good with people.

"Well," Darl began.

He lit a cigarette, the flame popping like a tiny piece of burning sun.

"My granddaddy played the pipe organ. Now that was something!"

He smiled, looking up at the sky as he smoked. Parnell was relieved. Darl spoke with enthusiasm.

"We lived in Huntsville until I was twelve, when Grandaddy died and we moved here. He left my folks a shop, like a curious sort of, oh hell, what would you call it?"

He looked to Parnell, who shrugged.

"You know, old flags, a display of gold coins, this crazy-looking fetus in a jar, that was I have to say disgusting. And a pipe organ. People paid."

Parnell tried to imagine the scene, tried to summon a film visual, but nothing came.

"I learned to play. I don't think it's in my bones though, you know? You can learn something but don't mean you do it well."

He dropped and squashed his cigarette.

"Mrs. Crank is coming back. She's the regular organist. Off to see her sister who had a baby, but she's coming back, so that's the end of old Darl at the organ. Maybe it will bring some folks back to church."

For a moment, Parnell thought his friend looked sad, as if he was admitting a great defeat. Parnell knew what it was to feel defeated.

"Well, I thought you did a great job."

Darl looked up and smiled. Parnell smiled too.

"Sitting up there in front of all those people, giving it your all. I think that's great. Nothing I could ever do," Parnell said earnestly.

"Yeah," Darl said.

"Where did all the people go?" Parnell said. "Wasn't much of a crowd for Sunday."

Darl shrugged.

"Somewhere else for church, I guess. The preacher, he's got a good heart. I like him. But he gets a little moody. You know. Not for everybody. Oh, hell. Let's go eat."

Parnell did not argue with that.

13

There'd been not a drop of rain for ten straight days. Darl and Parnell sat at a rusty picnic table outside the Sonic. Darl was on his lunch break.

"I thought I heard thunder last night," Darl said.

He set down his Chicken Slinger sandwich on a spread of paper napkins and looked straight up at the steely blue noon sky.

"Shit," he said.

"How did the preacher know?" Parnell said. "He predicted the drought in church."

He was sitting across from Darl. He could not fit his legs under the table nor his bulk if he tried to face forward. He sat facing away and turned sideways to communicate. Darl never seemed to notice or judge the struggles related to his bulk. This was a relief.

"I'd say he dreamed it?" Darl said. "That's quite likely."

The local weather had not begun speaking of the drought until several days after the preacher's sermon.

"Maybe he was just guessing," Parnell said.

A pickup truck rattled by on the two-lane fronting the Sonic. Across the street in an empty dirt lot were two teenage girls barely dressed, sharing a cigarette. Not far from them two same-aged boys hovered, folded within themselves, invisible, dark and lurking.

"Oh he's strange all right, our preacher," Darl said.

He was devouring the rest of his Chicken Slinger. Parnell nursed his Oreo Cookie Blast milkshake.

"I take it your Uncle Willy didn't tell you?" Darl said, standing to stretch, peering up again at the sky, then glancing at the teens. The boys had begun to edge closer to the girls.

Parnell, facing away for comfort, also watched the teens. There was the sheerest memory surfacing, this of a sexual nature, a coming-of-age film, skinny-dipping, fair and supple youth. But he wanted to focus on Darl, so he forced his mind and his girth to shift sideways.

"Tell me what?" Parnell said.

Darl had finished his lunch. He folded his arms. Parnell liked when Darl settled in to share a story or a bit of life musing. It made him feel special.

"I can't know for sure. But about a year before he died, your uncle that is, the preacher spent a lot of time out there. Old Willy had quit farming, quit the whole damn town really. Crazy recluse, we all said. So when the preacher started going, everybody figured he was sick. Looking for God. But that ain't right. There's something else that happened out there."

Parnell waited. The teens across the way were still as if they too were listening, waiting.

"It was the preacher that changed," Darl said. "A little bit at first. Then that summer before Willy passed on, it's like – Well, hell. It's hard to say. But it was like he took his brain and buried it away and got a new one. But that new one was broken. His sermons started to get weird. I gotta admit sometimes scary. He'd talk about dreams and nightmares, but then once he said a few crazy things that really drove folks away...."

The group of teens, Parnell noticed, were no longer two separate pairs, but one cluster of four.

"Sin and redemption stuff. But mean like. Anyway, folks didn't like it one bit and moved over to the church in Stantonville, about ten miles out. You know it had to be crazy to get folks to drive ten miles on a Sunday. But I always liked the preacher, so I stuck around. Like an old bug in a rug. Ha!"

He laughed at his own joke, and the bright sharp sound of it startled the four teens who were leaning into each other now like birds feeding.

"Gotta get back to work, Buddy," Darl said. "You want to go swimming tonight?"

Parnell was silent, unable to comprehend how that could happen, how he might swim in public, but Darl took his silence as a yes, and headed inside.

"I'll swing by around 8. They say ain't going any lower then 95 tonight. Wow shit!"

Darl was gone, inside the Sonic, and when Parnell turned back, the teens too had disappeared.

14

The first thing Parnell noticed was the water. It was a luminous dark green. It reflected the full moon and so many stars igniting the night sky. It was a large pond, two miles off the main road and down a stretch of gravel to a wide grassy shore. It was deserted.

Darl said it was a secret spot. Parnell wondered if wading in the shallow end might be cooling. He figured if he could remember where the pond was, and if it was truly isolated, he could come back by himself. He had not swum since childhood, not since he'd gotten so large. He did not know if he could stay afloat, and he did not undress in public.

Parnell wore a lightweight pair of sweatpants and a plain white t-shirt. Darl was at the pond's lapping edge undressing quickly.

"I got lost on my bike one day and ended up here. It was a while ago. I was alone, swimming out, and I swear to God I heard something splash, and I thought all of a sudden of that movie with the scaly guy, what's that? Aw shit!"

Trying to pull off his shoes, he fell backwards. He wrestled the shoes off, then yanked the pants and tossed them behind him.

"Anyway, that creature-feature thing, but I thought I best just wait because this is a good find and if I run now, I'll never be back."

Parnell stood watching from a few feet away. Darl had stripped naked. He stood up and turned.

"What ya waiting for?" he said. "You gotta be hot as I am."

"Go on," Parnell said.

"What are you scared of? It's real shallow the first few feet if you can't swim much."

Parnell thought of that film creature, any creature really, knowing he was the frightful thing here. Could Darl truly not see him that way? He didn't hesitate or flinch at the idea that Parnell might take off his clothes and reveal what lay beneath. Darl was watching him.

"It's been a long time," Parnell said. "You go. I'm gonna wade in a little."

Parnell slowly, carefully, sat and then removed his shoes. Darl ran into the water and dove, hooting.

Parnell, with steady effort, stood up and made his way to the edge. He stepped into the green water. The incline was very gradual like Darl said. He was in up to the ankle. The wet thick mud pressed between his toes. The soft coolness of it surrounding his foot in the water was immediately comforting, the caress a revelation. He had very few comforting sensations in his life. He took another step. The mud was thick and swallowed his feet. He stopped.

"How far before it's deep?" he shouted.

Darl was floating on his back. He flipped so only his head bobbed in the moonlight.

"Well, not too far. Can't ya swim at all?"

"I don't know."

His feet were sinking deeper into the cooling mud.

"Should I try?"

"Wait," Darl said.

Darl swam a frantic crawl stroke back to Parnell and stood at his side. The water only came to his knees and his nakedness was moon-lit.

"Can you do this?" Darl said.

He swooped both arms out in a V, making a circle, swimming in air.

Parnell sighed.

"Do you tread water?" Darl said.

Parnell was silent. Darl put his hands on his hips then sat down. There was enough water to cover him to the chest.

"Let's just sit then," Darl said. "Look at that moon!"

It was a risk, to sit, but Parnell took a deep breath, determined. He took his time, lowering slowly, then going back on one arm, then letting himself crash into the mud. The water felt very good in the heat. He was breathing heavily.

Darl leaned all the way back, submerging, then coming up again to sitting. Parnell did not, unsure if he could hoist himself back. He wasn't sure if he could even stand up on the unsteady wet and muddy floor. But he felt happy. And he felt free.

"Did you know my Uncle Willy?" Parnell said.

Darl did not answer. The night was quiet and still. Darl lifted his arms in the air, then began splashing at the murky water, causing a spray ahead of them. The movement made ripples which concerned Parnell. He was afraid it might unsettle the mud and unseat him.

"Stop," Parnell said.

Darl did. He sighed.

"I ain't a nosy person by nature. Friendly, but not pushy," Darl began. "Your uncle, I guess I'd say went through a rough patch."

"What does that mean?" Parnell said.

"You're a funny sort of man," Darl said.

"Yes, I know."

Darl had dropped his hands back in the water, but brought them out now into the air, lacing his fingers together.

"He's your family. I guess you ought to know," Darl said. "He just sort of went a little crazy."

"How?"

Darl pulled his laced fingers apart and held them aloft, as if he had a string balancing between his hands.

"There was a day at the Sonic," he said. "It was a week before he passed on. I saw his truck, well your truck now. It was in the lot. It was late at night. I kept thinking he'd come in. I find folks that can't sleep come to get food. We sell a lot of the mozzarella sticks at night."

"They are good," Parnell said.

"Well, that night, it was summer hot as it is now. He was out there I'd say an hour. In his truck. Sitting. So I went out, ya know, make sure he didn't pass out drunk or something."

Darl, who had kept his hands in the air, now let them drop back into the water.

"I heard the sound right away. But I kept walking. I thought of minding my business, but it was what's the word? Worrying."

"The sound?" Parnell said.

Darl turned and looked at Parnell, then looked away.

"I thought he had an animal in there. Something sick. Then I saw it was him. He was shaking. Crying. I shoulda stopped then, gone back in. A man is due his grief. Not my business. But like I said, it was worrying, the sound of it, so. I got to the window and I think he knew I was standing there, staring at him, but it was like a train gone off the track, it just can't stop before smashing up into something."

Darl sighed again. Parnell waited. He was aware how the water was surrounding them, protecting them.

"An old boy in town told a story once and said his woman was so sad and torn up that she was caterwauling. So, I guess that's good a word as any for it."

Darl stood up.

"I'm getting waterlogged. Let's go."

"Is that it?" Parnell said.

Darl shrugged.

"Yeah. He never looked at me. Just went on like that and I went inside," he said. "I guess you oughta talk to the preacher really. He knew him best. He spent time out there. I never found out what he was so upset over."

Parnell knew he could not stand in the mud without help. He wondered if Darl was strong enough, or if he'd just pull Darl down like a tree.

"I can't get up," Parnell said.

Darl turned and, without fuss, bent and hoisted him with a few loud grunts to standing. He was a strong man.

They stood together just staring out at the water, the moon high above. Then Darl stretched his long arms over his head and turned to go. Gingerly, Parnell followed, making it to the shore, following his friend back to the safety of the truck.

15

It was very early on Sunday morning.

Parnell stood behind his house, looking at the sprawling acres. The heat wave and drought had settled in and, as the local TV weatherman said, it would not *loosen its fiery stranglehold* until fall. Parnell had purchased a small television set and old-fashioned rabbit ears to pick up the broadcast. The weather was reported in a strange way, sounding more like a soothsayer's prophecy. The weatherman wore a plaid shirt and a bright tie and put a lot of emphasis on a lot of dramatic words. His name was Burl Tate.

Crops meant everything to this town, that was clear. They must have meant a lot to his Uncle Willy. Parnell wondered what had happened to make him give it all up. To go a little crazy, as Darl said. He would need to talk to the preacher. He would go this morning.

Looking at the land, *his* land, he felt a growing urgency. He had no vision for farming, but he had decided, maybe charmed by the mystical and dramatic tones of the weatherman, that something lay out there in the lost earth for him to find. Uncle Willy had given him the farm for a reason. It was, for him, a kind of miracle.

As he turned to go, he glimpsed, a few hundred feet out in the field, a flash of movement, something shadowy and dark.

Turning back, he saw nothing. He bent back his head, to see if a single cloud had miraculously appeared in the ceaselessly clear sky and cast a strange momentary veil, but there were no clouds. He waited. Could have been an animal.

The fields remained lifeless and dead. He turned to the barn to get the truck and head to the church.

He was used to the truck now, taking his time to wrench open the old tooth of a rusty door, stand on a sturdy metal box which gave him the leverage to hoist himself in. It was a slow, delicate operation. Getting out of the truck was a bit trickier. He mostly tumbled into the dirt, making sure not to land on his shoulder. He backed out of the barn and made his way.

He enjoyed driving down the empty two-lane, moving toward the relentless blue sky ahead. He felt he was going somewhere in his life, accomplishing something. Even if it was only to ask a preacher about his dead uncle.

The church's parking lot was empty, which he expected as it was so early. But he had a hunch the preacher would be there. Getting out of the truck in the dusty, rock-strewn parking lot was as expected, a chore. He took his time. After he swung the metal door open and slowly turned himself sideways in the cramped seat, he had a moment of panic. The distance between the seat and the ground was daunting. He'd tried a few techniques but found a small push-off, hoping to land steady, was best. Taking a deep breath, he pressed his hands on the seat and pushed his weight out. He landed on his knees, which was not too bad. He'd take his time getting up. Looking toward the church, he realized he was in a prayer position.

He did not pray, was not religious, but saw it as a good sign nonetheless. With effort, he got on all fours, and was able to slowly push up. He hoped the preacher was in the church. He didn't want to go through all of this again.

At the door, he caught his breath, then went in.

The man turned very quickly, nearly electrically, as Parnell entered. The preacher was in front of the altar. He made a loud hiccup sound, ran one hand several times over his forehead, then sat on the floor. He bowed his head and spoke.

"I knew you would come," the preacher said softly. "God says so much, the whispering you know. It's not a dream, it's a connection. But here I go talking about myself. Always talking about myself."

He smiled sadly. Parnell waited awkwardly.

"I can't really ever think of anyone but myself. Not the best thing for a man of religion."

He pointed to his head as if the trouble lay there, under that shock of black hair unwashed and tangled. He clasped his hands together.

"Can I tell you something?" the preacher said.

"Yes."

The preacher continued to hold his hands tightly together. It was as if he were squeezing something to death that was trapped in his palms. His hands were turning bright red.

"I wish you hadn't come," the preacher said.

Parnell took a step back. He'd made a mistake, broke apart some social grace. The man was a priest. He was invading his sacred turf.

"I just want to ask you about my uncle. I'm sorry."

The preacher laughed out loud.

"What I meant was I wish you'd never come to this town. That you didn't exist."

Parnell was taken aback. But Darl said the preacher knew things. Parnell spoke quickly.

"Darl said you knew him. Uncle Willy. Spent time with him."

"Well," the preacher said, laughing lightly, looking back at the ground. "You could say that."

Parnell took a few steps forward.

"Darl said you knew him pretty well."

"Is that what Darl says?" the preacher said. "He doesn't really play the organ very well. Our Darl."

The preacher turned quickly to the organ as if it would press out a note of answer, heave a cloud of dust to contest.

"And here you are. Wanting to know," the preacher said standing quickly, lifting his long arms over his head. "And what can I do but confess, here in this place, how can I do anything else? The stain of sin is relentless. Such violence can't be gotten rid of. Don't you think?"

The preacher stared at him intently, waiting.

"I don't understand," Parnell said, sweating in the stifling church.

"Are you sure you really want to know what happened to Old Willy?" the preacher said.

Fighting an urge to turn and go, to stop the stepping forward of any of this, Parnell nodded. Because he really did want to know. And he thought: *That's why I'm here. In this town. In this place. Something is actually happening to me.*

"All right," the preacher began. "We can't hide our sins from

God. Once I start, I will have to finish. The whole story. The most terrible part of it. And then you will take that with you. A violent death. A crime. Do you understand that burden?"

Parnell did not know what to say. He waited, wanting the man to get on with it. He wished he'd brought Darl with him.

The preacher moved back to the altar. He stood behind it as if ready to preach, then his put his palms on the surface of it. He mumbled quietly, then looked up, lifting an arm and indicating the front pew. Parnell sat.

The preacher folded his hands tightly together again. He shut his eyes and began loudly.

"It was all done and all hidden, buried forever. but I knew that was a fool's dream. Every morning the sky opens, burning us with this endless sun and damning heat, and when I feel the heat on my skin, I know what we did, Willy and I, and that other man. A life was destroyed. I can't say it any plainer."

The preacher lowered his arms, his shoulders dropping so low he appeared hunched. Then he looked out at Parnell and smiled weakly.

"I fooled myself into thinking God forgot, forgave. Nobody knew what we did, so it was all gone. Forever. Washed away!"

He said these last words not just with great emphasis, but with of an intensity of hope, as if he could hold those words high in the air here in this holy place and make it law. He kept staring at Parnell, and Parnell was moved by what he saw, the desperation and the fear.

"But then you came," the preacher said softly, resigned. "And I knew it was always there. The sin. Waiting patiently like a soul in purgatory. The quiet period had just been a lull. Like us waiting for a rain that doesn't come."

For a moment Parnell thought, this is too much. It's going to be too much, and I ought to get up and stop this now. But he could not. It was already happening; he was already in it.

"Tell me what happened," Parnell said.

The preacher left the altar, went to the pew and sat next to Parnell. He took Parnell's wide, meaty hand in his small, bony hand. He looked in his eyes and he said:

"I'll confess it all now."

PART TWO
WILLY'S STORY

PART TWO

CHAPTER SEVEN

There is light in this darkness and earth in my mouth.

The dirt settles everywhere like a blanket. Francine's blanket. That is one of my best memories. Those, all, a comfort really. The rememberings.

A thin skin of dirt on my lips, traces sifting onto my teeth.

My life was land, surely, as I was born here in this place, dug with gusto at this earth, planted, rooted, gave to, took from, thrived. There is a story in the land, always, and it can be told from under this gentleness of earth when one we loved, and then loved us, begins to tell it. We are, after all, only a memory.

Them telling about us unspools it out there, into the air, so it then runs down here into earth and through me like a train at night. Fast and sure. So I can tell it, live it. Share it now from this dark place.

For my telling, what matters is the summer of 1952.

A drought summer, a hot summer. Those three months. The rest, my wife Francine dying, good crops, lost crops. Blessings all. Thin spiderweb-like rememberings.

But those three months in 1952. That's the real need-to-be-told part. Which begins really with Francine. I best start there. She'd died a year before. 1951. It had also seen a drought, short but mean, then the storm came. A relief. They usually held on longer, the dry season. Not that year.

She was excited, went running, her frail bony body, that crazy happy laugh. Running out toward the barn, screaming back to me, "Come on let's see, come on the rain." I was determined to finish my oatmeal. I didn't like how she jumped that way, everything having to be her way and right away. So I sat a spell and took my time. Then the roar of the storm, like God's jaws snapped open with a dark, terrible scream. The thunder and of course the lightning. I never heard her shout in fear, never heard her voice again, which I miss the most. And I never ate oatmeal again. Never ate breakfast even.

She'd been by the barn, happy I imagine, when the lighting struck and killed her.

So there's that.

Which is what brought Phil. 1952. The next summer.

It was another long hot day, working the crops. He came on foot, moving up the gravel road toward the house. Taking his time, toting one scrawny suitcase. Stopping to dry his brow. It was over 100. I had taken a rest after a back-breaking morning with the men. I had an iced tea in my hand.

He saw me, paused for a short moment, then smiled and kept walking straight up the hill, straight toward me. I thought he must be selling something. I didn't see a car. Maybe he left it on the road. He stopped in front of me, dressed in a worn-out long-sleeved white shirt dusted with a film of dirt and brown pants and shoes. He was a young, good-looking man. Sturdy.

He set down the suitcase, which I gathered might have an elixir or some junk he was selling. He put out his hand. It was shaking a little, which was the only thing that told me he might not be quite right. After a moment, he let his hand drop.

"I'm looking for work," he said. "I heard about your loss. I'm sorry. I thought you might need a hand."

I finished my tea.

"I'm looking for work."

"You said that already," I said.

"The preacher sent me."

"He's got nerve," I said. "Son of a bitch."

This made Phil smile.

"Not a man of religion?" he said. "Might I trouble you for a glass of that tea? I've been walking a long time."

The straightforwardness of that got me. Didn't make me mad. I like a man who speaks his mind, and I right away imagined he might be an honest fellow.

"Come on," I said leading him to the house.

I did not ask him in, but got him a glass of tea and watched him from the kitchen window. With his hands free, he rolled up each sleeve. He took his time, made each fold even, then folded it up again until it settled neatly at his elbow. Like that mattered in the dreadful heat. Like anybody cared. But it said something about him. There was something I admired. I made my way out with the tea.

"Where's your family?" I said.

He drank the tea straight down.

"There's none," he said.

I thought, *That's not possible*, but I believed a man was due his privacy.

"I'm from the East. I worked on automobiles. I didn't like it.

I want to work with my hands. The earth. I'm willing to do any kind of job, even cleaning. I cook a little. I'm a fast learner. I'll work for room and board."

He'd started talking faster and faster, and I knew he was desperate.

"You worked a farm?" I asked.

"No. I'm hungry and broke and I'm a hard worker," he said.

Then he looked away, like the air had run out.

Funny thing, I believed him. There was something about him seemed trustworthy. Work can be learned, but honesty wasn't always easy to find. I was shorthanded. My crew came at dawn and left at night. There was plenty of space and too much quiet.

"All right," I said. "Is that all you got?"

He lifted his suitcase in answer.

"Come on," I said.

I led him up to the house and that was the start.

It was after dusk, and the men were drifting toward the barn where Phil and I sat. They were heading back to their homes for the night. Horace, big as an ox and meanest man you'd ever want to steer clear of, stopped, spit tobacco, put his hands on his wide fleshy waist.

"Ain't you two a picture of gentlemanly shit," he said.

He laughed. It was loud and coarse and even that was mean. He was a damn good worker, could hoist and throw and order the other men around and get things done. But his mean streak was relentless. He never had a bit of kindness, not even a look. He twisted words, spat them out like that nasty tobacco he was always chewing. Everything he said pitched things dark and angry. But I did not make it a habit of knowing or judging my men. As long as they got the job done.

"Better get in soon, gonna be some thunder and lightning I bet," he said with a big smile, turning to go.

I cringed. It was likely to rain, sure, but my gut said he added the lightning to get a rise, that meanness he had. I turned away from him toward Phil.

"He's peculiar," was what Phil said.

"You could phrase it that way," I said.

Phil smiled. He'd been working with the men for three weeks. And like he promised, he was happy to do anything. Scrub the kitchen, fix a broke-up chair. And he cooked like nobody's business. I never asked him how he knew to cook, but I was grateful he did. Roast pork, roast beef, chicken stew, fruit pies, a glazed ham. He could do it all. I'd put on five pounds. Mostly, it was good to have a human being in the house.

The night sky was clear and the moon big and bright. We shared whiskey. There was a soft distant howling.

"Do you think it will rain?" I asked.

"Don't know," Phil said.

The howling, likely a wolf, was a lonely sound.

"Can I ask you something?" I said.

"All right."

The drink had softened my edges and there was something in Phil that made you want to talk.

"You been married?" I said. "I lost my wife you know."

Phil took a long pull off the bottle, passed it to me.

"You could say that," he said, then after a long pause. "But it didn't work out. So, I gave up on all that."

A light wind came up and we could smell the tobacco leaves. Growing, they were fragrant, herbaceous, masculine, woody. Akin to jasmine. It was a nice scent. Not at all like the smell of smoking tobacco. It cast a gentle skin over the night, and I sighed.

"Only the one for me," I said. "We were good for each other. Guess that's it for me."

Phil looked over and smiled. He laughed lightly, looked as if he might speak, then didn't.

I held his look and I wanted to speak; there was something taking shape, but in feeling not word, moving around by that rushing smell of tobacco blowing onto me, onto my skin, under my skin.

I set down the whiskey bottle. I looked away.

We sat until the first sound of thunder, then went in for the night.

We sat around the kitchen table. It was crowded with food. The preacher smiled and bowed his head.

"Lord, thank you for this abundance. For this good food, these good men, their good friendship. We are grateful. Amen."

"Thank you, Preacher," I said.

"Call me John," he said. "Let's eat!"

Back then, before the madness set in, Preacher John was a bright, spry and cheerful man. He was wiry but very strong. His stories were funny and his sermons short.

"You are a gift to this world, Phil," John said. "Who taught you to cook like this?"

Phil smiled, but before he could begin there came a torrent of hollering, two angry voices then just one voice. Then nothing. It was Horace. Most of the men were gone, but a few had stayed for a drink. Horace's venom would break things up. He was a mean old cuss.

We paused, waiting. But no more shouting.

"I picked up things about cooking here and there. I traveled a while," Phil said, passing a bowl of fried okra. "It's a good thing to know. People always appreciate a good meal."

At my asking, he'd made a honey ham, then carrots, sweet potatoes, buttered rice and the okra. It was a spread. I was glad the preacher had agreed to come. I wanted to thank him for sending Phil my way.

"Do you drink, Father?" I said.

John winked and held up his glass. I brought out the whiskey.

We ate slowly, cherishing the food.

"Are you going to settle here, Phil?" John asked. "You said you are a traveling man. Maybe this is your last stop. You've found friends."

Phil finished chewing a hunk of ham, swallowed, drank.

"You make a good point," he said.

He looked across at me and we both laughed. Then John laughed too. It was a very bright time. Those days. We did not have to reach to be happy. It hovered over us and never blew too far away. It was a good season all around.

I was clearing the table for dessert, taking empty bowls into the kitchen. From the kitchen, I heard their voices:

"I guess I'll stay as long as Willy will have me."

It was Phil. I stopped at the sink, glancing through the doorway toward the two men, seeing their comfort and feeling an uncommon, peaceful joy in my body, my whole body, a gentle happiness that spread up to my chest, holding there, in a thrilling way, holding there and causing me to take a very deep breath, bringing a short spasm in my shoulders and a shiver that crept into my very mind.

I recalled, in that same moment, a sermon of the preachers about a spiritual ecstasy that some saint or other had felt. And I thought, standing there alone at the sink, *Is this something like that?* But it soothed itself away, the riled feeling drifted off, and I went out with the peach pie.

That was a week before the incident.

Through the long hot summer of cropping, a man's body, his very being, starts to feel like it's part earth. Made not of bone and blood, but earth. Dirt, leaves, stalks, scent – all of that is right on top of him, in him. Soon, it is him.

Me and the men are out in the field for months, dawn to dusk in them leaves, hands touching and yanking, tobacco stalks scratching ankles, calves, the smell of tobacco not just in your mouth but under your tongue and deep inside your skin.

Chopping, hoeing, cutting and stripping. Over and over. Month in, month out. It can change you. The mind can turn in odd ways.

Through the years, I found that by late June men started to shift. Some, like me, fall into a kinda trance. The rhythm of the long, hard workdays, the movement forward. Knowing a good end is coming. I know it will work out.

Others though, they tire. They go dark, get unruly, aggravated and a little crazy. I'd guess it's like being at sea. Endless ocean, day after day, night after night. Like the day to day world, those things that make us whole get swallowed up. Some men disappear about this time. I wake up with one less worker. I expect that to happen, just hope not to lose too many good men.

Round this time, when I get in my gut a sense the unrest is running high, we do a pig roast. That summer of 1952, it was the end of June. A Saturday night with Sunday off.

Phil and I spent half the day setting things up while the men finished their work. We hauled the kitchen table out to hold the food, which Phil made. We did it in the wide empty patch fronting the barn. A bit off from the fields. Despite the heat, we got the bonfire going. Mostly to scare up a smell other than tobacco. And to roast the pig. Men needed to forget the field, to get all that out from under their skin at least for a night.

There was plenty of food – and whiskey. Maybe too much of everything, but I always thought, *Hell, it's one night. Like Christmas in June.*

By dusk, they were coming toward the light of the fire where we sat. I felt proud. Happy. Each face that lit in the firelight showed childlike wonder. I knew it was a good thing. Even for a moment.

Except for Horace. He was one of the last to come and he had his own flask. I thought, as I saw his face, *Something's not right with that man. He's like the reaper.* But the firelight plays tricks. Once he moved on, I lost him in the dozen men who were laughing, drinking, finding the food. I felt good again.

The night was hot and clear. A scattershot million stars bolder than normal. By midnight a few of the men wandered off home, a handful stayed. Horace held court. And with the liquor, he got louder, telling stories and jokes. Taking charge.

Phil and I stayed a bit off from the fire, alone, giving the men their space to cut loose. But after a while, Horace, who was by the dying bonfire light with half a dozen men, set his sights on the two of us. He kept pointing at us, laughing then finally he started to sing:

"There once was an odd prancing fuck…"

He had a bottle to himself by this point. He took a long haul as the men drunkenly cheered him. He moved slowly toward us.

"An odd prancing fella, who really weren't nothing but yella," he sang.

He drank again, moving closer.

"He cooked and he cleaned like a bitch ain't been weaned…."

He threw his head back and laughed and I thought he was done. The men were quiet, waiting. Horace's shoulder slumped and his head lolled back, then it came forward. I saw in his face that same look I saw in the firelight when he first came, something darker than it should be, something awful. He began to move more quickly toward us as his song went ragged and off tune. Phil stood up.

"He thought he was something the fucker he thought he was better the cluck the pucker," Horace sang louder, moving faster toward Phil, knocking him down. I stood up, but Horace swung his bottle out at me. It sailed and hit me in the chest and I lost my balance, fell back. The men were watching.

Horace got down on the ground and was straddling Phil now, smashing his fist into Phil's jaw, then punching hard on his chest all the while singing some crazy gibberish. I hopped up and gave Horace a swift kick and sent him flying. Phil rolled over, holding his sides.

Horace was up again, yelling.

"We work all these years, back breaking and along comes this fuck and don't he get all he wants. A good bed, a place by your side like a brother and for what! He ain't good enough to lick my ass that fucker…"

As he screamed, as I saw Phil rolling in pain, there was a voice welling up in me, a rage I kept trapped and dark since Francine's death and something else, an older death I'd not let in the light but there it came, with a roar.

"You shut your mouth! You pack and get out now. Tonight."

I moved right up to him, face-to-face, and his eyes were black and burning and his breath stank and I wanted to throttle him, but I just yelled louder.

"Don't you ever come back. You are an evil man, Horace. I always knew that. You get out!"

My body shook and the men went quiet and Horace looked like I'd punched him in the belly. He backed off, but not in fear. I think it was plain shock that I had in me such rage. He stood stiller than I'd ever seen him stand.

After that, I got down and lifted Phil, hoisted him into my arms. I did not look back at the men, only focused on the weight of the ailing man I carried. He was moaning softly, then he too went silent and passed out.

As I moved toward the house, there was no sound at all.

Not of men. Not a grunt or a spit or a cough. Nothing but the fading hush of the dying fire. Then, as I struggled to open the screen door while I was holding onto Phil, there came the barely heard sound of boots on earth. Them all slinking away.

The door slammed shut behind me, and I put Phil on the dining table. I started to undress him.

He was out cold. Stretched across the big oak dining room table used for holidays. His arms were at his side, his head turned so one cheek rested at the table's edge. He almost looked peaceful. But there was blood seeping through his pants at the knees and more blood soaking the side of his shirt. Blood was also dripping out of one ear. These lines of blood crept across the table and onto the floor.

I did not know right off what to do. The doctor lived in town and it was too far to drive Phil, in his condition. Plus, the doc was a man known to drink himself to sleep nightly. I had to do this myself.

I had in my mind, for a moment, Francine at the doorway, hands on her hips. Holding something. I shut my eyes. She knew how to do these things. She'd mended my broken leg, splinted it before the doctor. Stitched me once. Wrapped my mangled hand. In the doorway there, she would carry something in her hands.

I felt unsteady and went to get a beer from the refrigerator. It was hot as hell. I drank. I went back. Phil hadn't moved. The blood was pooling fast, more lines making trails to different edges of the table and onto the floor.

"It's a satchel," I said aloud.

A medicine bag, in the bathroom, under the sink in a cabinet that had no door handles since they'd rusted and I'd ripped them off, threw them out. I got the bag. Francine's mending bag. I opened it, and it was like she breathed a ghostly sigh of relief on my neck.

Rows of bandages, tape, alcohol, swabs, some red liquid, an eye dropper for what I did not know. A sewing kit. It was well organized. She was that way. Thoughtful and prepared. I looked up, but there was no shadow in the doorway, no whispering voice. Phil turned his head and opened his one un-blacked eye.

"I ain't dead," he said.

Then he laughed, but winced at that effort and shut his eyes again.

"I'm gonna take off your shirt," I said. "You want whiskey?"

He didn't say a thing. I began.

The shirt had been torn a bit in the tussle. Getting it over his shoulder (which had a long scar I'd never seen) made him moan and getting it out of the arm holes surely hurt since he grunted and grit his teeth.

The shoes came off easy. The pants gave me a problem, since his one knee was a mess. I unbuttoned the top, then brought his dungarees to his thigh. His underdrawers were very white and I wondered how he got them so white, a strange thought at the time, but it made me ashamed that my own clothes never got much attention. I stopped the pants at his thighs. I was leaning over the table, hovering. I wondered if I should climb on the table and straddle him and try to yank. The table was old and might not hold two men. I knew whatever I did it was gonna cause real pain to get his pants over that bad knee, but it had to be done. I looked around for a knife to cut them off.

"Just do it," Phil said. "Like a bad tooth."

I took a breath, got a good hold and pulled them down over the knee. He didn't squeal. Which was impressive.

I went to the end of the table and yanked them off over his feet and threw them into the heap of bloodied clothes on the floor. He let out a loud, ragged sigh, and I figured he must have been holding that back, like a badge of courage. Who knew how other men thought in moments like these? If it was me, I'd yell as loud as I could for as long as I could.

"I ain't no doctor," I said.

"Go on, and whiskey," Phil said.

There was none in the house. It was all outside. I figured after getting all the taking off done, he could use a break.

I went out through the screen door to the pit, which was still fired with embers. The roasting

setup holding the part-devoured pig. Litters of cans and plates. I spied a bottle and grabbed it. Turning to go, I wondered if it had been Horace's bottle. Had he sucked on it, spit in it, left his venom there.

I moved fast back to the house, spooked by the high bright moon and far off cries of animals and emptiness of the stretch where the party had been.

When I got in, Phil was snoring. I set the whiskey on the floor. I had Francine's mending bag open. I looked over his long body. Horace had done a lot of damage in a short time. He was a strong man with fists that knew their way to pain. I was guessing he'd done a lot of this sort of thing.

There was a big purple bruise on Phil's abdomen. I touched

it, leaned close as if I could hear inside. I decided that would be all right. I ran my hand slowly up his flat belly, to his chest, thinking if there was a bone out of place or something, I might feel it. He was not like me. He didn't carry fat like I did, and he didn't have much hair. I'd not had an occasion to see other men much. Not going in for sports or the like. He seemed a healthy man.

I knew I had work to do. I just wished I knew how to do it. I figured the knee was the best place to start.

He lay on his side. I turned the knee gently and Phil let out a yelp, like a bit dog. There was a hunk of skin gone, like Horace had bit him, though I know he couldn't have. There was a lot of blood and that raw underside of skin and dirt, bits of glass. I wondered if I should look for the lost skin, but thought better of that and decided to wash it, clean it, and bandage it for tonight.

I went to the kitchen, found a pot, filled it with warm water and found a towel.

"Sorry, Phil," I said.

Before I started, I lifted his head so he could take a few drinks. Then I set his head back on the table. He sighed.

I was as gentle as I could be. Dabbing, washing the spot, squeezing out the towel, changing the water, doing it all again until it looked a little better. At least the stray bits were gone. I had to lift his leg.

"Phil," I said.

He was silent and I figured he may have passed out with the pain, which was a blessing. I thought of the preacher. I could have called him. He seemed like the type that might help out late at night.

I needed to lift his knee so I could wrap the bandage around, which proved difficult since each time I lifted and tried to wrap, his leg fell back. I went and got a sofa pillow and put it under his calf, then pushed his foot up a little, so his knee stayed up leaving space for the bandage. I centered my shoulder on the table for leverage and leaned my face close to his thigh and set into wrapping.

He had a scent to him. Like his clean clothes, he had a scent of pine soap; and while I wrapped, I was thinking how I'd stopped caring much about something so particular as pine soap since Francine went. My mind was not my own that night, twisting away from me. I got the wrapping done and I was tired, and in a strange way, comforted there, my face leaning close, taking in his scent, and I wanted to shut my eyes and stay there, but of course I did not. I went and lifted Phil's head for another drink. Ends up he was wide awake. I held his head up for another moment. I gently set his head down.

The gash in his head was for show, not as bad as the blood made it look. I bandaged his cuts and washed him, and ran my hands on the large purple bruises once more, in case a bone had found its way up, though what I'd do about that I did not know. By this time, he was out again. It was deep night. I dare not move him. I fetched a pillow and a sheet to put over him. I watched him there, sleeping, breathing lightly for a spell.

Then I shut out the light and went to bed.

I slept long and hard without a remembered dream. I woke happy.

It was Sunday, so things were quiet. The men were gone until dawn work Monday. Phil slept through the day. I thought of waking him to see if he wanted the doc or to move to his bed, but decided to wait. Sleep heals.

Just before dusk, I was frying an egg in the kitchen when I heard him moving. I'd found a carved walking stick and left it by the dining room table where he was spread out. I figured he'd need it.

I shut off the stove burner and went out. He was already sitting up, in his white drawers, both legs over the table side.

"You did that," he said indicating his knee. "Thank you."

I went over and got the stick and handed it to him.

"This oughta help," I said. "You want clothes?"

He smiled.

"In this heat. It's still Sunday, aint it?"

I nodded.

"Egg?"

He shook his head no.

He had the stick in his hand, but I saw he was fairly unsure if his knee would hold. I went and gave him my shoulder. One hand on the stick, the other arm draped across my shoulder, we moved a bit. I got him to the kitchen and put him in a chair by the window.

"Eat your breakfast," he said.

"It's night," I said.

"Oh."

I ate.

All wrapped up, his knee didn't look half bad. I finished up and put my dirty plate in the sink.

"How's it feel?"

"Like shit," he said. "Everything been through a grinder. But I'm all right. I guess a drink of something."

I got him a beer, opened it, put it in his hand.

"How you get your drawers so white?" I said.

I sat in a chair across from him.

He drank a lot of the beer fast. There was a line of foam around his lips.

"Bleach."

We sat for a while and I got him another beer. And one for me. It got later. There was no need to talk about the night before. Men would likely show up, get to work, say nothing. That's how things were. Nobody liked Horace much. He wouldn't be missed.

Dusk left and evening came on, the way it does in summer. Slow, gentle, like maybe it's not coming at all. Maybe the light will stretch on and on. Then all of a sudden the sky is full of stars and at least a little edge comes off the heat. I didn't turn on the light. It was nice to just let the darkness be. I got us another beer.

"Thank you for what you did," Phil said softly.

"I don't know if I did much of a good job on that knee," I said.

"Not for the mending. For scaring Horace. I think he meant to kill me," Phil said.

I sat across from him and noticed how he was looking at me. Serious, but calm. I could tell he believed what he said.

"Why in the world would he want to kill you?" I said.

Phil did not look away. He drank his beer. He kept looking

at me. He smiled.

"It wouldn't be the first time," he said. "I don't know if I can really explain it. What he saw in me. But I could tell he was set on getting something done. Getting rid of, well, like I said I've seen it before."

He finally looked away and sighed.

"You think you can get me outside?" he said. "I bet there's a breeze out there."

He was right. The kitchen held heat, and if we were lucky, there might be a half-assed breeze or something close to not stifling.

"You ready to travel?" I said, then laughed. "Hell."

We finished our beers, which gave me a minute to get past a sense I had that he was talking about something other than what he was saying, which was a strange feeling to have to begin with since I didn't know quite what I was even thinking. Still. I wanted to say something, about all that with Horace, but the words weren't there. Something else surely was there, but at the time I couldn't let it in.

"If you think you can make it out," I said.

He stood up, using the walking stick. I left the side door open from the kitchen and gave him my shoulder and we went out toward the back. He was moving pretty well. There was a soft howling now and again, and he was right. The air was a little cooler outside.

"Let's go into the field," Phil said.

"Why?"

He laughed.

"I don't know. I like it out there. I guess I never told you that. You might think I'm not right. But I like being in the field. With the tobacco all around me."

He said it in a matter-of-fact way, but also like he was sharing a secret. Like it was special. I liked that about Phil. I believed what he said and knew he did not doubt the things he said. I realized, too at that moment, moving him slowly toward the field, that I loved that place too. The crops were my life, in my blood, part of me. Not because it had to be, but because I wanted it to be. We got into the crops and the howling came again, then a second and a third time but different voices, animals from distant places maybe reaching out to one another. It all seemed close. I was wondering if Phil's knee might give out, but he seemed not to be too bothered.

"Here?" I said.

He was leaning a little harder on me.

"A little further. It's like going deeper in the water. Getting out to where you feel like there's nothing else."

"I like that," I said.

And I knew, as we moved a bit further, that we were in a good spot before he said it. We were completely surrounded by the tall tobacco plants, the thick leaves big as a bear's paw, the short hairs on them oozing tiny drips of yellow. It was like being out at sea at night. Lost.

The stretch of the sky above looked wider and more endless than normal and it didn't feel so hot and it didn't feel quite real. With the howling, there were night birds flocking by too, though I couldn't see them. Just heard wings flapping. Phil was leaning on me. He let go of his stick and it fell to the ground.

"You think I'm crazy?" he said. "Wanting to come out here?"

I looked out across the long stretch of big veiny ancient-looking leaves that went on and on.

"No," I said. "It's good."

When he leaned his head in close to mine, it didn't occur to me that anything was wrong. We'd been standing close for a bit. We were of similar height and the closeness felt natural as I held him up there. When I felt his cheek on mine, I first felt it was all still the same, all part of the same walking, talking, being; but as his cheek stayed on mine, something else started and I felt it clearly and I became afraid.

"This is a good place, Will," he said.

His voice was so close, his breath was there. It was like he was in my ear telling me something and I choked up because it was a good place, it was my life, so many years in this field, this place, but now it was different. All at once, it was new. There were more sounds, the animals, and more birds, but all I wanted was for Phil to say something; to feel his breath and for something to keep going on, and I was already past the point of thinking, of striking anything down that hadn't been part of what I was just in the kitchen.

He turned himself to me and we were even closer, and the brush of his lips were there and I was there, but I was part somewhere else, because this didn't seem to be happening to me though it was.

Phil was still leaning on me to stay up. The hand across my shoulder was now on my cheek and he said something soft, but I didn't hear it clearly, and he let his lips move from my cheek and brush right near my lips, and I thought, *Well, here it is*. And it was then, not a surprise, rather something forgone but now here.

Just like the first time I felt how rough the leaves were on my skin, a finding out but then feeling that I'd already known.

Phil was leaning more on me and I felt him tremble and I knew that his knee was giving out. We went down onto the earth, together so he didn't fall, and we sat side by side. It was safer down there. Like in a hidden room, but with a sky. And there was nothing in the sky mean or awful. Nothing watching but the beauty of a night sky.

We were leaning into each other and that was nice. There was moonlight. I unbuttoned my shirt, got an arm out. Phil laid back. I got the other arm out. It was still so hot. I got easy out of my pants and lay down too. Side by side, like we were ready to sleep.

There was a whip-poor-will cry and I smiled because I knew it was the male, making a fuss, which they did in spring and summer at night. It's a far-off, high-pitched sound. A music that has movement in it.

Phil sighed, then turned and put his hand on my belly. I had that sense of being in night water again, and things were getting slower and slower. He ran his hand from my belly up to my chest, then side to side. I touched his belly the night before. I did that. Just like that, mending him.

He did that now a few times, and it fit with the rhythm of that whip-poor-willows song, rising then falling, over and over, and the leaves too, moving in a repetition with the bits of wind. His hand kept trailing, and I sighed with him, long and low; then I did what I'd never, ever imagined. I pulled him up on me and I kissed the man. I had not seen this, dreamed this. No. It was not part of anything of me, but here it was and then I knew what to do.

Our kiss was long. We were facing one another by now, the kiss went on and his hands trailed on, then mine did too and I stopped thinking all together and the heat didn't matter and I didn't even hear the bird any longer, just felt my his our wandering touch and then his lips away from my mouth onto my chest and belly, and things came along like they were coming together, without a fuss, just on their own, and the night had a rush and a flow and the sweat didn't matter much and it was like this: it was what I didn't know I had but that I had been waiting for, for such a long time.

And then we stayed there, cradled, all night.

I woke, dawn coming up, and the light soft song, that churree of a swallow. The sun cut into where we were and the shroud of night was gone. We were naked, legs overlapped. I didn't want to wake him, though I wondered how he slept on with the mounting brightness and the rising heat.

I wondered that his knee hadn't started to ache him. I didn't want to move though. I wanted to stay being what felt like part earth, down under, not of the world quite yet. It was too early for the men to come to work. We had a good two hours. My bones felt stiff.

More birds sang, but also a strange sound, hard flapping, like rushing wind over and through the tobacco leaves. But the longer it sang, a harsh song, my mind was afraid again and then I knew it wasn't wind and it wasn't right, it was something else and it was coming closer.

Before I could stand, the sickle was slashing into the leaves near us and through the cutting leaves he came and there was nothing to do but look into those horror-struck eyes and see the rage and glee and evil. Horace lifted the sickle over his head. He didn't move. He just looked at us. Men naked in the dirt. He held the blade in the air like it ought to scare me, but it didn't. I don't know where my courage came from in that moment. But it came. I had stepped into something of myself that would never be gone now.

"Get off my land," I said.

At that, Phil moved a bit. He was rousing.

Horace, that sharp thing still hovering over his head, the blade reflecting a cutting sun, laughed out loud, though it was a forced sound, a mean laugh.

"So now we know!" Horace said with a terrifying glee.

Phil was waking and trying to sit up.

"Get," I said as loud as I could. "Get off of my land."

He brought the sickle in front of him and it dawned on me what he'd been up to. Destroying my crops. Killing what was mine. Taking his revenge.

"Your Francine never gave you a son. Look at that. Now we know why. You sick fuck."

He hawked and with force spit on me. The big wad hit my chest and spilled slowly down one side.

"Willy," Phil said softly, almost like we were still alone.

"You musta disgusted her to the bone," Horace said. "Killed her. You killed that poor woman."

Then that awful loud, long laugh again, and my eyes were blurred and my mind blew open with Francine, like the lightning that struck her could have been my hand, and I knew that was not true, not true, but he was making it turn that way, and I would not let that happen, and the rage of last night was nothing, this was far more fierce and horrible, this rage and reckoning would not be turned into something that I was not, was not, did not kill my wife, I would not feed it and it would note be real fueled by his evil. As he turned away talking:

"I got your balls in a sack now. I got a story to tell!"

I stood and flew at him.

He's a fat man, that Horace. Strong but-heavy footed, and when I grabbed him from behind, it startled him and he yelped and I got one arm around his gullet and I pulled my arm back with a wrenching force like I was tearing the lies out of him and I heard something crack and he was trying to make sound but he couldn't, and Phil was at me, trying to pull me off, but I was steely bent on destroying this wretchedness, and then it was too late and Phil yelled so loud and I let Horace's body fall to the ground with a mighty thud.

I hauled the body in a wheelbarrow into the house. Getting him up into it was like hoisting a big bag of meal. Phil with his knee could not do any lifting. He gathered our clothes and hobbled behind me. We put Horace, with his neck broken and dead, into the bedroom. We shut the door and drew the curtains.

We washed together, and I helped Phil clean and rebandage his knee, and we stood under the shower water and held each other, and I knew this was how it would be now. This thing had forever joined us. Nothing could break us apart. And then

I thought how I had just killed a man and the sin of it and the retribution that would surely get me. But I did not quiver with fear or regret since my rage at Horace was still bright hot, and I did not care that I would surely pay for this moment in life or in death. Gripping Phil's naked back was unlike anything dreamt of and so full of its own grace and wonder it blighted my surely seen and judged evil.

So I held Phil tighter and thought over and over, *Nothing can break us apart.* And that somehow felt bigger than anything else. Bigger than a dead man lying in the room. Bigger than my sin. Bigger than us being not possible.

We had found each other, and that could be nothing but beautiful.

The men came and went to work. Nobody asked about Horace. He'd made a scene, and it made sense he'd leave town. Nobody would have expected him to come back. We went about what we always did and nobody ever went to the house, so we weren't worried about that. But then somebody did come to the house.

Around noon, the preacher showed up. Like I said, he'd come for dinner before, and since then he might stop in for a beer or to borrow something like wire or a tool, things he might not have at the church.

Phil and I were in the side yard. The preacher parked and was whistling and heading to the front door. We went fast to stop him. Phil slowed because of his bad knee, but I went straight to the front door and stood in front of it. Preacher John paused. He looked at each of us, then said to Phil:

"What happened to your leg. And your face?"

Phil was dead still. I saw he was struggling with the pain.

"Phil?" the preacher said.

Phil was wavering in the heat and I saw him going down. I ran out to him, but he fell on his side and yelped as the fall musta hurt his leg. I kneeled by him. The preacher came over and knelt down too.

"Let's get him in the house," the preacher said.

I looked straight at him and I thought, *Those are the eyes of God.* And I thought, *This is a chance here. To give up. Or be struck down.* Then I backed away from that and got my arm under Phil's and the preacher did the same and we helped him into the house and into a chair in the kitchen. Then we all stood there. I realized how very tired I was. Finally, Preacher John spoke up.

"Do you want to tell me what happened?" he said softly, kindly.

He looked at me again and I couldn't help but think of the eyes of God, of Francine, that lightning bolt which always spooked me, that fate. Phil lowered his head on the table and again I thought, *Nothing can break us apart.* I nodded to the preacher and walked to the bedroom. I opened the door.

He was at my shoulder. We stepped in.

Horace was splayed out on his back. It was clear he was dead. His eyes were still open. He looked unmarked. The preacher walked slowly over to the bedside. He touched Horace's wrist, then his heart. Then he knelt and began to quietly pray. I stood at the door, not knowing what to do. The praying went on a bit. Then the preacher stood up and looked at me.

"Did you do this or did Phil?" he said.

"It was me."

My whole body tensed up like a man in battle.

The preacher intertwined his fingers. He made odd sighing noises. He looked up at the ceiling then down at the floor. He sighed again. His voice was ragged. Louder. He looked at Horace as if he were speaking to him.

"I saw this coming. Last month. Just like this. In a bad dream. Lying on his back, eyes wide open. But one hand was reaching up. I thought, 'He's gonna die,'" the preacher said.

He bowed his head again and I waited, wondering what to do. Then he started talking again.

"I figured God was testing me. The man scared me. I'd heard about him. I knew he was a bad man. Very, very bad. People had told me about him. Things he did. His badness. I went out to his house. To talk to him. I figured that was my job. To try to save him. Evil can change."

I looked back to see how Phil was. I figured the preacher needed to get this off his chest, whatever it was, though the timing seemed strange, being that we were both staring at a dead man.

"He lives way out," the preacher said. "Away from folks. When I got there, I got out of my car and I was scared. I wanted to run. All my strength was gone. He came out, he spit at me and laughed. He had a woman in the house. She was yelling at him. He cussed at her. Then he turned fast and cut into me. He had a vile tongue, he said horrible things about God and the church and me. He came at me drunk and mean, and I got in the car and drove away as fast as I could and never looked back."

His voice trailed off and he shook his head, mumbling a

little. Finally, he looked back at me, smiling weakly. But his eyes had changed. I swear to God they'd changed. They were not so clear now, they were different.

"I'm a weak man, Willy. I never had to face much really. I do all right with the church. But then God tested me, and I failed. Failed miserably."

He turned to Horace.

"And now this. Now this."

I saw him struggling and that didn't seem right. This was not his thing. He didn't kill the man.

"You can leave. I'll never tell anyone you were here. Just give me some time," I said. "This ain't your problem."

Then I added: "This ain't your sin."

Phil had made it to the door. He was right behind me. I could smell him. I wanted to touch him.

The preacher looked at us.

"I don't know. I need to pray. Can you leave me here?" the preacher said.

We stepped back and shut the door. We went into the kitchen. He was in there a very long time. He didn't come out until it was night.

PART THREE
RAIN

1

Parnell shifted in the hard pew, uncomfortable. It was very hot and he was very hungry. He had listened to the preacher's long disturbing story. It was not at all what he expected. His stomach had growled a lot and his head had throbbed as the history hurtled toward its violent end. While he truly wanted (and felt obliged) to know what happened to his uncle, he had wanted to suggest they take a break. Maybe the preacher could tell him the rest later that evening when it was cooler. But he'd said nothing. It was clear once the man began there was no turning back. He was a renegade train careening downhill. Even as he spoke of himself at the end, he did not hesitate. Parnell did not dare interrupt this strange telling.

Sitting now, considering what he'd heard, he had no reason to believe it wasn't true. The preacher seemed a bit unbalanced, but he'd told it as if he were living it, with such vivid detail and sureness, Parnell did not doubt him.

Parnell tried to imagine his uncle now, to hear his voice, but he could not. None of it was what he'd hoped for. Nothing was comforting.

The preacher was still seated by him with his head down. His shirt was drenched with sweat. Parnell thought that maybe if he put as much vigor into his sermons, more people would come.

Finally, the preacher looked up, weary.

"I'm sorry," he said.

"Why?" Parnell said.

"Does it help you knowing all that? I am supposed to help people. I can't seem to do that. I told you for selfish reasons. To rid myself. To give it over to you. It's yours now. This terrible history. The truth. You have no choice but to take it."

The preacher jumped up, as if the pew had caught fire. He stared at Parnell.

Parnell pressed his hands on the side of the pew to rise. He'd sat too long and needed momentum to get solidly up. He certainly didn't want to fall, or worse, stand too quickly and topple onto the wiry preacher. Taking his time, Parnell stood, facing the man. The preacher took Parnell's hands into his own.

"It is all yours now. Do you understand?" the preacher said.

Parnell took his hands away. He had not thought of it that way. None of this had existed a few short weeks ago. He had been solidly, safely alone. But now that the words "It is yours" were said, they seemed to hover in the air and take shape. To circle him meanly and with a dark assuredness and purpose. He was afraid.

"Do you think you can save us?" the preacher said. Then more softly, "You have to. Please."

Parnell stepped away. His mind blurred.

"Well, I'm going to go now," was all Parnell could manage.

He moved as quickly as he could without stumbling down the aisle. He felt an urgent desire to flee, as if something he could not see wanted to swallow him whole. The preacher followed, keeping a close pace, speaking quickly, so close behind.

"The crops failed for Willy. After that, nothing grew. The land is bad. Ruined. It's a curse that you can break. Don't you see?"

Parnell was halfway up the aisle but turned, already out of breath, knowing he could not get away from the man.

"See what?"

The preacher grew calm. He spoke slowly.

"Horace is buried out there. On your land. I helped them do it."

For a moment, with the altar's cross behind the preacher as if it were rising out of his skull, Parnell saw the man, and it dawned clearly on him that this man was part of a murder. It was not a story. It was a crime. The telling part, with Willy and all, had felt stray and different and away from anything real. But now, the preacher staring at him, close to him, confessing his part, it struck Parnell very hard and he began to tremble part from hunger and part from this realization, and that cross behind the man's head, it was all so much bigger than he imagined, too much for him, a man who had come to this place to escape a dreary life, to take on a farm, who had nothing to lose, who had no one who loved or cared for him or needed him. This was going to be his chance. It was his one tiny possible moment at something meaningful in a sad dreary life. But this part was not good. Willy and Phil and Horace and the preacher. It was not good. And now he was part of it. He was part of the story. A story of murder. Bones in a field. He had not asked for it, but it was here. As if listening in, the preacher spoke.

"It's up to you now, Parnell."

He had to go. To get away from this man. He had to sort this out.

Parnell turned without a word and made his way out of the church. The preacher did not follow him this time.

2

Before him: a SuperSonic double bacon cheeseburger, jumbo popcorn chicken, chili cheese tots and a Coke. And Darl.

On the drive over to the Sonic, Parnell grew ravenous, dizzy and disoriented. His brain could not fully connect what he had heard in relation to where he was in his life and this place, this land. His *obligation*. He had to eat.

He and Darl sat at an outdoor metal picnic table. Darl smoked.

Halfway through the meal, Parnell paused. He could breathe again. The air was strangely still. As if things had stopped, which in some ways for him they had. He needed to tell Darl what the preacher had said.

"I talked to the preacher," Parnell began.

Darl dropped and stubbed his cigarette. He stood up and began to do a toe-touching exercise.

"I think I best get in shape this summer," he said. "Let's swim tonight."

Parnell took a gulp of his Coke. He began again.

"He told me some strange things about my uncle. I'm not sure how to say it."

Darl did not pause his exercise.

"Let's face it, he ain't all there. I like the preacher, but you hear his sermons?"

"It's more than that," Parnell said, then he belched.

"Sorry."

Darl stopped his exercise, but not because of the belch. He was looking at something in the distance.

"Well shit!" he said. "We got us a dust devil!"

"What?" Parnell said. Turning he saw it.

It was a gray funnel-shaped mass spinning up to the sky. *Like a tornado*, Parnell thought, *but more contained, like a white-gray whirlwind shooting to heaven.* It was in the distance, but moving toward them quickly.

Darl hooted.

"Well shit, I ain't seen one since I was a kid," he said.

Parnell froze with fear. He was not a person who could move quickly in the event of danger. He could not descend narrow staircases to dark root cellars as they did in Kansas in a black-and- white film, or run from things as he'd seen in so many films. He was doomed. He thought, *I have heard this cursed story and now I am cursed. This is all really happening. This is the thing I came for. I wanted something to happen, I wanted to feel alive. This is it.*

He felt too the terrible aftertaste of the preacher's story, the fate of his ruined uncle imprinted on him now, in his very blood; he, the descendant, the chosen one to carry on the awful curse if only momentarily before he was sucked skyward then likely dumped onto his inherited farmland, maybe on the very spot where Horace was buried. And for a moment he thought he saw a face in the funnel speeding toward them, heard a screaming voice.

He struggled to stand.

"It dies fast, don't worry. It won't get us," Darl said.

He put his arm across Parnell's shoulder.

"I shoulda told you that first. It's all right. They just pop up in summer."

Parnell was shaken, but the touch on his wide shoulders, the so-foreign bit of comfort, along with the fact that indeed the funnel was suddenly and rapidly sifting downward to nothing, calmed him.

Parnell sat. He picked up the popcorn chicken. The dust funnel was gone.

"How could that be?" Parnell said.

Darl was back to his toe-touching exercise.

"It ain't like a real tornado or anything. Happened during a Little League game when I was eight. The kid who was catcher. It just caught up right where he stood, knocked him over, spun out to first base and died."

Parnell kept eating.

"Well, gotta get back to work. Swim tonight?" Darl said.

Parnell could not launch into the preacher's story now. But he had to tell Darl. He felt everything in his life had at once blown apart and strangely come together.

"Come by my house," Parnell said.

"Roger that!" Darl said, dashing back into the Sonic.

Parnell looked toward the place the dust devil had been born and died. He kept staring until he finished all of his food, then he got into his truck and drove home, keeping an eye in the rear-view mirror, expecting, perhaps, the ghost of Horace.

3

They were out in the scarred tobacco field under a scattershot of stars. They were lying on the hard ground. Darl had brought a cooler of beer. Parnell asked Darl to forget about swimming. He told him he had something important to talk about. He'd had time to calm his mind. He was pretty sure Darl would have something to say about the preacher's story, that he could help him make sense of it.

Parnell did not normally lie in the dirt. It was too hard to get up. But Darl had lay down right off and started in about how great the sky looked, and Parnell did not know what else to do. He would need to speak up. There was a trio of night sounds. A fast and constant high pitch, a lower growl that bled into a croak, then a darker third noise he could not quite figure out. The sounds were ceaseless and loud. Darl didn't seem to notice, but then he'd grown up in Kentucky.

Lying quietly, trying to think of a way into the story, Parnell listened. The sounds of deep country held mystery and wonder for him. He had grown up in a juvenile correctional facility and then a cramped room for rent in New Jersey, both which echoed the roar of nearby highways. An orphan, he'd been sent to the correctional facility because he had once, only once, fought back when he was bullied (he was nine but quite large, always large).

He had fallen on top of the bully in a tussle and nearly crushed him to death. It had not been good. He did not want to tell Darl any of that. He did not want to tell him he'd never known his parents, that he'd never known Willy.

Parnell cleared his throat. He began to repeat what he'd been told by the preacher, and as he spoke, his tongue loosened, the story gushed forth. He did not need to think, and he lost any sense of shame or worry. It was as if possessed. The details were there as if lived. He was not sure how he'd remembered it all so clearly. He figured it had to do with being in the very field where it all had taken place.

When he finished, he sighed, waiting. He studied the night sky.

He heard Darl opening another beer.

"Well, I'll be damned," Darl said.

They sat listening to the tree frogs sing, the insects cry. Parnell craned his neck to see his friend lying near him.

"So, he's out there, that fucker Horace," Darl said, sweeping one arm across the horizon.

He hopped up quickly.

"Or right here! He might be under us, for shit's sake."

Parnell had not thought of that.

"They would have buried him further out. Not so close to the house," Parnell said, struggling to get up into a sitting position.

Darl paused then sat again and drank.

"Makes sense."

Darl made a noise, like a hum. He did not form words, he just continued to make a noise from his throat. A growl, almost like one of the night creatures.

"You know what I think?" Darl said, standing again.

Parnell waited. He wondered if he should get up on his knees, to start the process of standing.

"Parnell," he said, turning to look at his friend. "A man's got his own business, and it sure as hell ain't mine to know. I respect that. You never said why you came here. You never said nothing about yourself."

"There's not much to tell," Parnell said.

Darl turned away and began to pace slowly. It seemed to Parnell that Darl moved as would a lawyer speaking a truth, building a case, as he'd seen in several films. Some black-and-white.

"I always been nosy. I'll tell you that," Darl said. "I right off thought why's this guy here? What's he want with a farm? That's just natural thinking, I believe."

As he paced, his feet brushed tobacco leaves, this hush adding a theatrical air. There was moonlight and it illuminated him.

"I believe in ghosts," Darl said. "I heard 'em. But that ain't important. What I'm getting at is I think this, this story you had told to you, I think that's why you are here. I think you gotta change things here. Make things right."

Parnell was struck by the similarity in what Darl said now and what the preacher had said.

"This land is poison," Darl said. "That's why things stopped growing. Maybe that's why your Uncle Willy died. You gotta fix that."

Darl paused. He looked out at the acres of night. He stood

taller. Parnell felt a lightness growing, a feeling of hope. It was a thing altogether new.

"What should I do?" Parnell said simply.

"We gotta get the preacher out here to bless it. To make it right. Then I think you need to bring this land back to life."

"I don't know how to do that," Parnell said.

At this, Darl knelt down.

"You own a fucking farm, man; you know how many people dream of that from around here? The land belongs to you. It is yours. But you belong to the land too. Like having a kid."

Parnell was moved further toward that light called hope now, a light he could identify, not by the ideas or the thought of doing any of what Darl was saying, more by the simple fact that Darl spoke with passion about something concerning him.

"All right," Parnell said.

"Come on," Darl said.

Parnell began the slow process of getting onto a knee, then another, so he could build up to standing. As he did, he felt the earth on one palm, another, one knee, another. He had an urge to taste the dirt, to lick a finger. Since it was his earth.

"Where are we going?" Parnell said.

Darl, still looking out at the black acres,

"To get the preacher."

4.

They sat in front of the church for a good long while. There was a light on, but they did not go in. They sat in silence, sharing a wonderment of what they hoped to begin, though still unsure how to do it. Finally, the preacher stepped out. He lit a cigarette and, in the match flame, spotted them. He ambled toward Parnell's truck. He smiled.

"You fellas out late," he said. "I was working on my sermon."

He seemed to have shucked the terrible angst of the storytelling, to have forgotten it.

"We want to show you something," Darl said. "Out at the farm."

At that, as if a cloud had obscured the moonlight, as if a phantom had descended, the preacher's face went dark. He dropped his cigarette.

"Can I fit in there?"

There was a lean space behind the front seat. Darl opened the door, got out, then pressed himself back there like a child. The preacher got in up front. Parnell drove.

"Does this thing have a radio?" Darl shouted from the back.

The windows were wide open to the night's unbearable heat. A hot wind tore through the cab. There was that cry of the night, the rustling things, but it was a blur in the wind itself.

"Forget it," Darl yelled, settling back.

At the house, the three stood staring at the dead field. Those worn, wretched leaves, the aftermath of something long gone, with shreds holding on. The moon was bright.

"Come on," the preacher said.

The old tobacco field stretched a good way back toward the acres beyond, but as they went, it died out slowly, leaves and even wild weeds giving up so there was nothing but earth. A good ways back, the preacher stopped, looked up at the sky, then at the house, then sighed.

"This is it," he said.

"What," Darl said. "How the hell?"

The preacher was calm, which surprised Parnell after all of that dark telling. Parnell was spooked. He felt they'd started something unstoppable, and it frightened him. His initial sense of discovery, of having a purpose, felt strange and fragile out here in the dark field.

"Willy used to sit right here like he was keeping a vigil, or maybe making sure old Horace didn't rise out of the ground," the preacher said.

"He sat out here a lot. At night. All year long. I sat with him a time or two. Especially toward the end. I thought he might want absolution. He didn't."

Darl knelt down in the dirt and placed his hand on the ground.

"So here?" he said.

"Yes," the preacher said.

"Well, shit!" Darl said. "I figured you'd bless the land or something. Like throw some holy water. Hellfire. Now what?"

"I think we should go inside," Parnell said.

The preacher turned to him. He reached out his hand. This unearthing of the confession changed the man. He wasn't so unhinged.

"We need to dig him up. Bless the bones. Give him a proper burial."

Parnell stepped back, shocked. The man said it with such matter-of-factness.

Darl stood up.

"Make sense to me. You got a pickax and shovel, Parnell?"

"I think we better go inside," Parnell repeated.

He paused. He had no reference point, no old or new film that showed this sort of thing that other people did. There was nothing in his mind but misgiving. Yet the two men were so sure. Parnell looked out at the land, his land. Then he looked at Darl and at the preacher, and he knew this was the right thing to do. And he was not alone. They would do it together.

"Let's go inside. I can make coffee. Then we can look in the barn for shovels," Parnell said.

He turned and began his slow walk toward the house, hoping they would follow. They did.

5

They came upon three shovels in the back of the barn.

What caused Parnell to stop abruptly was not that they were lined up perfectly in a row against the wall (something he'd seen in a film from 1980 about a field, though it was ultimately about an alien). What caused the immenseness of his body to quietly spasm in the stifling barn heat was a sense that things were moving so quickly, as if ordained, set in motion by something far beyond his control, something he had never experienced before.

The drab pain of his ordinary life had been remarkably replaced by something uncertain and frightening and thrilling.

Darl grabbed a shovel. He left the barn. The preacher sighed, then slowly took a shovel. Parnell did not know what to do. He would not be able to help. With the heat and his inability to do any type of exercise, certainly not to pierce some hard dry earth, he would be useless. Still, he took up a shovel and followed them.

The two men were already in the field, at the place the preacher believed was the burial spot. They always moved more quickly than Parnell. Looking toward them, he wondered why some men were spry. Indeed, they looked like wiry scarecrows in the field. He wondered if he brought a chair to sit in, if that would look too strange.

"I will go get us water," Parnell yelled, heading toward the house.

"Beer!" Darl yelled back as he lifted the shovel over his head and swung it down into the merciless earth. The preacher was saying something Parnell could not hear. Likely instructing Darl.

At the door to the house, he set down his shovel and glanced up at the hot and unforgiving night sky. There was, strangely, the appearance of a small gray cloud far in the distance; though it could be a flock of birds so far off to appear as a cloud. The drought was expected to hold on for a good while longer.

He went in for the supplies. He found an old cooler and some ice and beer. The cooler was on wheels. It was red and ugly and old, but it moved. He began to wheel it out to the men. The moon was bright.

He reached the place beyond the lost and withered tobacco plants.

"You're sure this is where he is?" Parnell asked.

"Yes," the preacher said with finality. "We need to go slow and steady."

The two continued to poke and press at the hard dry earth. Parnell had left his shovel over at the door. Darl began to sing. It had a religious slant to it, but he seemed to be making up the words and he hummed through long stretches. The preacher worked in a rhythm, stabbing, pausing, stabbing. Parnell's legs hurt. His feet had swelled. The men worked, paying him little attention.

He went back to the house, got a kitchen chair and returned

with it.

The men made slow progress. Darl opened a beer and sat it on the ground. Parnell put the chair a few feet from them and sat. No one seemed to notice.

He looked up and saw a line of clouds in the distance cutting across the horizon. It was odd, as if someone had colored a thick slate-gray line across the black highway of sky. He looked back at the men. They had removed their shirts and were sweating. But they did not stop. They pressed on. Parnell was hot, but lulled by their movement. He was very tired. A lot had happened in a short amount of time and now these two men, strangers such a short while ago, were digging up his future. Like a story unraveling that he only recently realized was part of his destiny. He smiled. He'd never had a destiny. It was not a word he used.

He looked up again at the sky. The bank of dark clouds had gotten fatter and were inching closer. He thought of the film with the birds on the jungle gym, each time she looked up there were more. He heard the crack of a beer can opening.

"Whew!" Darl said.

"Clouds," Parnell said, pointing.

Darl turned, drinking.

"They ain't nothing. They say the drought's going on another month."

Darl kept digging.

The clouds were thickening, growing like a living thing, multiplying. Each time Parnell looked away then back, more pieces of the horizon were filled, small patches of night sky disappearing behind clouds. Parnell heard the sound of the shovels stabbing earth, but he kept his eyes on the moving clouds until they had slunk their way closer and closer, bigger and bigger, then were above, then over them, overwhelming the entirety of what had been the sky. There was a shard of lightning, a roar of thunder.

Both men stopped.

"What the hell?" Darl said.

With that, a deep, bass growl and an instant and massive downpour came, as if the long and seemingly endless drought had stored a world of water that it finally let go.

The heavy rain blew sideways at a slant, an endless wall of water that appeared both separate yet one, heavy with a downward gush but also a million single drops racing in lines, in their pattern of direct and linear movement. It swept west to east ferocious but with grace, *the way dancers might fly cross a stage*, Parnell thought.

He could no longer see the other two men, only the rain wall. The dark prowl of thunder came again. Parnell saw everything as if through blurred glass and could still not see the other two men, nothing but this rain.

Lightning pierced and thunder belted, then came a new onslaught and a heavier wind. The gale hit him with a force that shook Parnell. He feared he might topple over. He had fallen before in a storm. Flat on his face. Then, just barely, he could hear Darl whopping and howling with pleasure. Parnell also heard a long steady screaming voice in the storm but knew it was likely his nerves.

Then as quickly as it began, it abruptly stopped. It simply was no longer. He could see them now, both men drenched, as he was. The preacher on his knees, head down, Darl dancing. Then they all stopped. The heat was back with force.

"Well, that was like a fucking miracle, right, Preacher?" Darl said.

He crouched and pressed his hands on the earth. Then he used one hand like a trowel, digging into the muddy ground.

"Only top layer got soft. Too much rain too fast," Darl said. "Don't do us much good."

He stood up and the preacher nodded in agreement. Darl's hands were caked with the wet mud, and as he reached to swipe sweat off of his brow, he left a dark slash like war paint.

The two men set into the slow, steady work of piercing and digging the tough ground. As they steadily worked, the top layer of wet mud splattered up onto their pants and arms, and working, wiping sweat, they each increasingly had slick stripes of dirt on their arms, chest and faces. It gave them the look of ancient warriors.

They dug and dug, grunted and sweated. Parnell shut his eyes, also drenched with sweat, trying to summon a film image about the end of something and the beginning of something new. But nothing came.

Finally, having dug the hole deep and wide, together feverishly working for a good long spell, they came upon what they were looking for.

"Holy shit!" Darl shouted.

Parnell wondered if they were waking an ancient rage.

Having stepped into the hole, disappearing, the preacher now reappeared, rising up, holding, with reverence, the skull of Horace.

6

They laid the bones on the kitchen table, but it was not long enough, so it was only half of Horace. His leg bones lay in a pile on the floor.

The preacher had carried the bones in several trips and set them in place. Darl was too spooked to touch them. The preacher arranged the bones as best he could but got confused in the refiguring and, in the end, lay some pieces in a line on the table with the skull. It did not look much like a human being.

It was late. They'd never had dinner. Hunger barked and riled at Parnell as it always did, but it would need to wait. He looked at the man's remains on his table. He wondered if they should have taken him to the barn.

Suddenly, the preacher spoke.

"God, bless this man who was struck down!"

He lowered his head and prayed softly. Darl kept his distance. Parnell watched. Finally, the preacher looked up.

"Well, friends, I think the thing to do is get these in a bag and I can take them to the church graveyard."

Darl stepped back further, nearly out of the kitchen.

"There's a graveyard?" Darl said.

"A few unmarked graves behind the church. Come on, get a bag, Parnell. Let the healing of this wretched man, of this land here, begin."

Parnell had trash bags under the sink. It was hard for him to bend without tipping over. He was feeling a little dizzy.

"Darl, can you get a few bags there under the sink?" Parnell said pointing.

Darl did not move. The preacher fetched the bags and began to load the bones. Parnell watched, and when he looked up, Darl was gone. He'd left the room. Parnell marveled at the preacher's fearless energy. He appeared revived. From somewhere in the house, Darl yelled.

"Is the drought done?" he hollered. "You think we brought the rain?"

The preacher looked up.

"Everything has changed," the preacher said. "There is no turning back."

Parnell's mind was a muddle.

"But what does this all really mean?" Parnell said softly.

Still bagging, the preacher spoke again.

"You need to bring this farm back to life, man. God has given you a chance to right a wrong. To redeem Willy. Let all this darkness die. Bring back the land. Can't you see that? Why else are you here?"

The preacher finished the job with the bones, then went out and loaded them into his vehicle and drove away, saying nothing else.

Parnell sat at the kitchen table. After a bit, Darl crept back in and sat across from him.

"Glad he took them old bones away," Darl said.

His body shook and he wrapped his arms around himself,

yelping a little.

"Creepy shit," Darl said.

"You think we can make things right?" Parnell said, considering the preacher. "Do something good with this old farm?"

Darl looked up without a beat.

"Yes, sir, sure as shit we can. We're in it now, Buddy."

He smiled at Parnell, and Parnell smiled back. There was a stillness in the house, a gentleness which Parnell imagined was what a *home* felt like. Maybe, he thought, the change the preacher had spoken of had already begun.

From a distance, in the fields, there was the sound of more rain and then a low, howling wind.

PART FOUR
WILLY

Bones shift. The mean one gets up a lot, restless. But now, the voice on the wind is all light, not dark, ashes and whispers. All mine. So, the part missed, not told to anyone, not seen by them there, can be told. Might as well get to it. It will find them.

It was good after we buried Horace. Sounds strange, but it was. Holding a terrible secret alone can be unbearable, but a shared one, no matter how ugly, is near tolerable.

We were in each other's skin after that killing, Phil and me. It was a bonding that started that night, lying chest to chest. But it grew bigger after what we did to Horace, no more just our fear of being caught. We had killed and buried a man. We were deep in that, no turning back, and it made us like one. Our fondness made us bold. We'd get on with life. We'd survive. This new connection, born of high sin, made us hungry for each other and fearless in protecting what we had.

Nobody seemed to mind Horace being gone, which was a good thing. I figured it was on account of his being so mean, that vicious way of his. Into summer and fall, the crops were good, the men content. But that's not what I'm telling now.

It's when winter came and the men left until spring crop. That's the part that matters.

We were completely alone. And things changed. Slowed

down. Got close. Not just sex, something deeper.

I never experienced anything like that. I guess it makes sense to start in the tub.

Winter had clawed its way in with a vengeance. Long bitter cold, shales of hard ice sewn in a mean wind, everything flying, snow piling and a far-off scream like winter herself saying, *Settle in. This is my time.*

It was a Sunday and we decided against church, with the brutal cold and high drifts (we went every week since we did the burying, since all that with the preacher). We shivered in the kitchen that day. No matter what, woolens, fires, liquor, a man could not get warm.

"I'll get us a hot bath," Phil said.

He stood up and, despite the cold, took off his wool cap, unbuttoned his flannels and stepped out, bare naked. He was a lean man and pale, sinewy hard from work and a softness I knew already. But his dark hair had grown longer, and in the winter light like that there was something that shook me more than usual. Maybe it was the daylight. We always laid together at night. I'd never thought to myself how beautiful a man can be, this man, here. Like I said, our lives had been twining but, in that moment, it was like he was all mine, I his.

I stared at him and he let me and I took a long deep breath, but before I could stand, he turned and went to the bathroom.

The tub was big and claw-footed. I heard the water running. It was a gentle sound, almost like a creek running in spring, and it calmed me, since the siren scream of the wind went on and on and was unsettling. For a fast second, I thought it could be Horace, howling for revenge. I did have nightmares. What murderer doesn't?

Steam crept from the bathroom doorway. It was heating up and I figured I best get to it.

I undressed quickly and shivered a little more with knowing what was just beyond that steam. My skin went goosebump and I moved fast to the doorway.

Phil was already standing in the tub as it filled, steam rising and surrounding him like a fog. I wondered how he stood the water if it was that hot. There was a lot I didn't know about this man, and mysteries I suppose I never did figure out.

I slowly walked to him and lifted my leg and put my foot in first, then got in the tub standing across from him. The first touch of water on my cold foot was like throwing on a warm blanket when you wake up at midnight realizing the weather dropped to freezing. It was soothing. Not as hot as I thought from all that steam. Maybe my feet were half frozen. We stood across from each other and Phil smiled, then turned off the water.

"How you want to do this?" he said.

I felt dumb, and excited, lost for just a moment, hot now with a strong need to reach out and touch him, but he just smiled with a long-held knowing I did not share. It was like every touch was new to me.

"You sit first. Take your time."

I did just that. It was like heaven, settling down into that hot water after so much freeze. I spasmed a little and sighed so long and loud it made Phil laugh. I was looking up at him now as he was standing, and I had that urge again to reach out.

His face was serious and beautiful to me and he turned,

lowered himself, and settled between my legs spread so we both fit, my back against the tub back, his back against my chest, his cheek and all that wild hair just near my mouth, and I opened my lips and took some of it in and thought this is him, his taste, this is what the men can't know we are.

He sighed and said my name real soft, and I reached around and rubbed my hand across his chest back and forth. The water was holding its heat and the steam was still hovering. That ice wind still screamed but sounded further off with my head and heart pounding.

He turned himself around somehow and found my lips and we kissed like that, then he sat back between my legs but didn't lean back, just sat up and I put my hands on his shoulders, rubbing. Then, caught off guard with a rush, I wrapped both arms around him and pulled him as close as two men could get, pairing in a tub, and he said my name again, and from there it was like sailing straight over whatever wildness we had been hovering at, and we turned into each other, awkward twining, pressed so tight in that small space, water moving all around us, our lips and mouths and hands set in, and we touched and we touched and that was how the best of it all started.

The rest of the winter, those long days and nights, they were like that. There was a sweetness to it, I'd call it that. Something I'd never had. My life with my wife had been a good one. Hard work, love there. But nothing that shook me open, nothing giving me so much at once like with Phil. It's hard to explain. Like being out in the crops working hard and losing all track of time and something touches your neck, maybe a raindrop maybe the wind, and you look up like time leapt away and you notice its full-on night and there's a moon staring at you and for a moment you think, *Well, that's really something*. It's a feeling of brand-newness, like a moon was something special. That's how it was with Phil and me all winter. Things going so fast, but too, moments that came on so bright, so filled up.

But then came the rodeo.

It was late spring. Men back, long days, hard work.

The rodeo came, just like the county fair, once a year. I never missed it. It was like being a boy again. I got that excited. Phil said no, but I kept bugging him, asking over and over until he looked at me in that way, stopped dead in his steps, really looked right at me, giving me that small slow smile, and then he said, "All right," and I thought he almost sounded sad.

So we went in May, the very first night. It was warm.

The fair grounds are just outside of town. Bleachers circling a big dusty bowl of a center ring with white gates going round the corral where the animals are kept. That night was tie-down roping, team roping, steer wrestling and my favorite, the bucking broncos.

It was a red sky night, but not that soft red, it was much darker, angry. All that sunset red seemed to get deeper and deeper. Like dusk was not letting go and the sky was bleeding for it.

Plus, Phil was antsy sitting next to me. He kept getting up then sitting down. He set to rolling a cigarette, which I'd seen him do a million times. But it was like his hands didn't work, and I swore they were shaking. He gave up and stood to watch the first act.

It was a good crowd, people yelling and kids crazy-acting. We had a good seat close to the action just above the cage where the rider was striding his horse. It was saddle bronc, not bareback. I was sitting. Phil had his hands on his hips and was rocking side to side, but I left him be and focused on the cowboy in the cage.

I could see him leaning back on the animal, hands on the ropes, frilly chaps and big cowboy hat tense and ready for that moment when the cage door flew open and the horse went wild.

The announcer yelled and the door opened and out they went, the horse's back legs flying in the air over and over, like he was kicking at all of us, the rider on him holding steady with the rope reins, legs tight. Two other fellas on horseback circled nearby so when the rider fell off, they could distract the horse so the man didn't get stomped.

As he rode, one arm flew in a circle by his side, balancing him, the whole thing for us, just man and horse like one lightning dance.

It was a damn good ride, then he fell off and rolled past, and we all thrilled for that split second when we wondered whether he would he get a hoof in the head. We all sighed like one, and it was on to the next.

I looked up smiling. I hadn't noticed Phil had left, in the fast and furious excitement.

I found Phil sitting outside near the entrance to the main show space. He was alone on a bench with his head in his hands. He looked terrible. I waited, thinking I best turn back, give him time to wrestle with whatever it is he was troubling him. In truth, we hadn't done a lot of talking about the past in the time we knew one another. I didn't know much about him really.

Not far from where he sat was a whitewashed tin booth selling fried dough and caramel corn. A large woman with a frizz of hair, a low-cut blouse, nursing a cigarette, was alone in the booth, watching me. She waved. I moved toward Phil. He lifted his head and I sat down. Then he started in:

"I figured we shouldn't have come," he said. "I guess I knew it would go wrong. There aren't that many traveling rodeos. But you seemed so happy."

He looked up and smiled and lifted his hand as if he were gonna touch my cheek, but then he let his hands drop and went on.

"The short of it is I killed a man. So Horace weren't the first."

From the stands nearby, the announcer's voice rang out. Steer wrestling started. There was a frantic excitement to his voice, which seemed odd hearing it next to Phil's steady, sad tone. Before I could think of what to say, he went on.

"He rode bulls. I groomed horses. We had a thing, you know, like us here, but not as good. Not at all as good. But a man needs companionship. That fella though..."

At this Phil stood up. He put his hands in his pockets, then he looked over at the fat gal watching us. She waved again.

"You boys want some caramel corn?" she yelled, and winked. She drew on her cigarette, adjusted her tight blouse. "Are you two the fried dough type?"

Phil turned his face to me and a darkness was there, like he was showing me his own deep red sky, a spreading out of loss and grieving I hadn't seen before. I knew something in that very moment had changed for him. We stared at each other and that worn-out look he had held steady.

"It's pretty easy to hide out at a rodeo. We're all just getting by. We had a good thing for a bit. Better for me, I guess. Just a thrill for him. That's how he put it when I asked for more. I guess he got spooked. He turned on me. Made a threat, you know, gonna tell everybody. Gonna say you tried something with me. He just wanted money it ended up, but it's like it hit me in a way I couldn't control."

Phil sighed and sat down again. He turned to me. The announcer rang on. The big gal watched, as if she could hear what Phil was saying, as if we were the sideshow for the night.

"What can I say? I went a little crazy. I didn't want to let go. He pulled the knife, but I was the one left him for dead. I always been a good fighter."

Phil looked up at the sky. He stood still for a long moment.

"Then I just ran. What else could I do?"

He paused, looked at me.

"Then I found you," he said.

I looked at him and I understood. I saw myself in his place and thought I might do the same thing. I think killing a bad man, like I did, makes you see life from a lot of angles. I had no right to judge.

"An old boy in there recognized me. Small world, rodeo folks. He'll be coming for me. Asking questions. It won't be good for either of us."

We were standing alone real close and even though the big gal was still watching, he took my hand, held it then kissed it.

"I think we best go," he said.

He stood up and walked over to the food booth and I followed him. I walked very slowly, trying to figure out what to say, or whether I should tell him we need to sit down here, smoke a cigarette and sort out what this means.

He turned and had both fists full of fried dough. He just barely smiled. I went up to him and he handed me one, then we walked to my truck.

The next morning, Phil was gone.

My heart broke and never healed. It was the end of me, in short.

How much more can a dead man tell you?

PART FIVE
THE FARM

1

Parnell had a strange dream.

It was the type where it seems not to be a dream, rather a waking moment, as if an actual dream has just ended. But then a realization comes that it is indeed still a dream. This was clear in the dream to Parnell because a ghost sat at the end of his bed. "I am Horace," the man said, and in the dream, Parnell knew this to be true. It seemed very right and beautiful.

Horace sat with his hands in his lap. He was heavyset, red-faced, tangle-haired. He wore a clean pressed blue jean shirt, a pair of tan work pants and was barefoot. Parnell thought, *He is so calm. Maybe that's what death is.*

Horace began to speak.

"The reason, which you guessed, is I have seen a lot. Looking up from the grave."

Horace sat very still, his hands not moving, talking in a low, calm voice.

"I won't go into how this all works, and what I do under the earth, but I did not rise. I settled mostly due to the life I lived. But lying, we get to watch, them like me, year after year, and we get a sort of well…"

He paused, lifted one hand to rub his chin in what looked like a rehearsed moment. In the dream Parnell also thought,

This is very calming, like a nice hot bath.

Horace went on.

"What you already know is I ruined things for Willy. Poisoned the land. Just shit it all. But you see, my friend. I hope I can call you friend? Like shit turns to something good in the earth, so do we, and that is what time is really. So, I better get to the point. The land is good. You need to farm it. So, that's it."

Oddly, even though in the dream Horace evaporated, Parnell dreamt further, thinking about what the man said. Things moved slowly in the dream. But finally, he woke, and it was all momentarily crystal clear to him what he needed to do. But he was immediately afraid. He struggled up, looking for Horace. He looked toward the end of the bed, then under the bed, then in a closet, then in the living room. It took him a while to settle down, to know it was only a figment. After a bit, he calmed his mind and went outside.

He went around to the side of the house and despite the heat, and his hunger (it was way past time for breakfast), he rubbed his chin (thinking of Horace in the dream) and surveyed the wide expanse of dead fields, wondering how they had looked when ripe and planted, bright and alive. He thought he might see the visage of Horace appear in the field, but he did not. He studied the long stretch of ratty and chewed-up acres and his mind, as if traveling out of his body, moving swiftly (which he never did because it was so hard to move) sped across the field and scattered like seeds a series of thoughts: *I have had no home, I have had no family, I grew up untethered and alone, and now I have land and I have a home and I have a friend. I need to plant this land. Like the ghost said in my dream.*

His eyes were scanning the fields as if following those thoughts, and he felt a certain freedom. He stood there for a while, thinking about everything that had happened since the day began, and he went in to get ready to go and see Darl.

From: The Step-by-Step Guide to Growing Tobacco, Independently Published

Tobacco is a plant that is grown for its leaves, which are used for making tobacco products such as cigarettes, cigars and chewing tobacco.

Seedbed Preparation: Tobacco seeds are tiny and require a fine, loose soil for good germination. The seedbed is typically prepared by breaking up the soil and adding organic matter such as compost or manure.

2

They sat outside the Sonic at a metal picnic table. The one with the umbrella. Parnell had his lunch: the Hickory BBQ Cheeseburger Combo with chili cheese fries, pickle fries and a strawberry milkshake. Darl smoked.

"Well, it's just about time," Darl said slowly, then smiled and slapped Parnell on the back, which nearly made him choke.

Parnell had told Darl about the Horace dream and his desire to make a go of the farm. He shared the book he had bought at the local store about planting. He did not, for maybe the first time in his long, uneventful life, feel doubtful or ashamed. He trusted Darl. He also knew, since facing the tobacco field and feeling his body lift off the ground and fly freely (in his mind at least), that something absolutely new was happening in his life. He was on the precipice of something grand.

Looking at Darl, and beyond Darl, at the waves of heat on the highway and the boxy cars that sped by and the hills in the far distance, he realized that the nagging certainty that all people hated him was no longer hovering, ready to strike. *And maybe,* he thought quickly, *it won't come back.*

"So how much money do you have?" Darl said.

He stubbed his cigarette and stood up, stretching. Parnell wondered if he started smoking, if he might eat less. Parnell could not raise his large arms over his head.

"I just have the farm," Parnell said.

Darl lowered his arms and turned and looked at his friend.

"You came here with nothing?" he said.

"Yes," Parnell said.

Parnell waited for the familiar voice to speak up, to shower him with fear and shame about what he had just said, but none of that came. Maybe it was because he and Darl had dug up a dead man.

Darl paced toward the Sonic, then paced back.

"All right," he said. "Then I gotta ask you something, friend."

At this point, Darl looked cautious, almost afraid. He had never seen Darl look like this before. A truck rattled past, then a car pulled in and parked, and a woman in stretch pants and a halter top, wearing a large sun bonnet, got out of the car. She slammed the door and moved dramatically toward the Sonic.

"Hell," Darl said. "Hold that thought. Customer."

He went into the Sonic.

Parnell finished his lunch. He was still hungry. The metal bench was uncomfortable, but he needed to stay put and wait for Darl. It was hard to stand, especially after eating, and to then reposition himself back down onto the narrow bench was a real chore. Most seating was not big person friendly.

As he waited, he realized he had stopped filling moments like this with scenes from films. This was a rather monumental change for him. He could not entirely grasp it, this string of changes taking place one after the other, but he knew they were the cause for a new sense of hope. He had never thought of himself as a hopeful man.

The woman in the stretch pants came out carrying three food bags. She got into her car and sped away without even glancing at Parnell. Darl came back out. He lit a cigarette, smiled and began again.

"Now listen here, you crazy fucker," he said.

Darl did not cuss much. So Parnell wondered what was coming

"I'm gonna tell you something."

Darl took a drag, blew the smoke.

"The day you came to town, and I saw you, and you being so big and everything and, sorry, but looking like you didn't know shit about farming or anything really – I sort of lit up with this idea that there was gonna be an opportunity for me to do something in my life. I mean, you got a farm and I thought he don't know shit and I thought I bet I can get in on this."

Darl paused, then sat down. He was closer to Parnell now and he spoke more quietly, a little less theatrically.

"It wasn't like I wanted to screw you over or something. I just thought," he looked down, "I live in a trailer, Parnell. I work at the fucking Sonic. I ain't done shit in my life. And I don't know, I guess when I saw you, I thought I bet he ain't done shit in his life either so the two shits sort of came together in my head like, hey, I think something good's gonna happen here."

At that he laughed out loud. Then he slapped his hands together.

"And holy hell if something didn't happen. I mean, there was the bones and all that, the bad stuff, but there's this now, you buying that tobacco book and you who don't know shit, thinking you can do something and you telling me. So…"

At this he paused. He went to yank out another cigarette but stopped and sat back down.

"I want to do this thing with you, Parnell. I want us to do this."

Parnell was transfixed by the story, this story that took that new feeling of hope and lit it on fire. He said:

"How we gonna do this?"

Darl smiled.

"I'm glad you asked, sir, because it all kind of came to me just before that gal came to buy her lunch and going inside gave me a breath to say, 'Yes, Darl, this is the right thing.' You see, I ain't much, but I own a trailer. I can sell it. And I saved some money since there ain't nothing to do here and I ain't done nothing with my life. And I figure if I move in with you and we partner up on this, well, we can figure it out and maybe hire some men and well, I guess start us a farm. Then we both can have something. We both can have something to be proud of in our pitiful fucking lives."

At this point, Parnell could not help himself. He reached forward and wrapped Darl in a hug, not worrying he might injure him in the doing, and he held him and he began to cry. And Darl let him hold him like that. Darl didn't seem to mind at all.

From: The Step-by-Step Guide to Growing Tobacco, Independently Published

Sowing: Tobacco seeds are sown in the seedbed either by hand or by using a mechanical seeder. The seeds are sprinkled lightly on top of the soil and then covered with a thin layer of soil or vermiculite.

3

They were outside, facing the expanse of field. Their future.

Darl had set up a low table from the house and two chairs, a tall stiff oak kitchen chair for him and a bigger living room chair for Parnell which he'd wrestled out. He thought it was important that they were outside, facing the field while they interviewed the men.

"If we get lost, we look out at the field. It will remind us."

Parnell was afraid, fearful of what the men would think of him, the bulk of him in that silly cheap living room chair like they were setting a scene in some outdoor theater.

But once they started, once they faced the first man, he was glad. He glanced over at Darl in that hardback chair, a notebook and pencil in his hand like he had something to write. And he looked out at the field, and it did give him a sense of importance, of reason. Even the small table was a barrier between them and the men they interviewed for the jobs.

It was early fall. The weather was fine. The drought, which had turned the town and the county sour, had vanished, and days were bright, rain came and went, things were tame.

The first few men had little to say. They just wanted work.

"Can you manage a tobacco farm?" Darl asked.

They repeated they just needed honest work.

The fifth man that came pulled up in a bright red pickup with jacked-up tires and a blaring radio. He took his time ambling toward Darl and Parnell and stood a little to the side. He did not sit in the chair placed in front of the low table.

Before Darl could start, this man, who was tall and young and well-built, wearing an extremely large belt buckle and lizard boots with a fine shine, started in. He had a toothpick in his mouth.

"What do you two think you're doing?" he said.

Darl looked at his empty notebook, like he was checking something. Parnell did not look at the man.

"What kind of question is that?" Darl said. "We aim to bring this farm back. Ain't that why you are here."

The man smirked, put his hands on his hips and took a slow turn, giving his back, surveying the land.

"You work at the Sonic," the man said.

"Not anymore," Darl said.

It was at that point that Parnell saw Horace. Out in the field. Far off. Past rows of scarred leaves. The Horace of his dream. He glanced at Darl, thinking to say, *Do you see that out there?* But he stayed quiet. In the distance, Horace was moving his lifted arm left to right, left to right, like an umpire. The man with the big belt buckle began again, still facing away.

"These crops are gone. I don't know where you two got the idea you could up and be farmers. This hasn't been a proper farm for a long time, and there's no way in hell you can just make up your minds and..."

At that point, Darl stood up so fast he overturned his chair. His voice was loud and ragged, near to a scream.

"You get the hell out of here. Get off this land. You get away right now!"

The wiry whole of him moved fast around the table toward the man, and the man, taken aback, also moved away fast, avoiding Darl like a bullfighter dodging a bull, and as Darl ran at him cursing, the man fled back to his shiny red truck, looking properly startled at the smaller man's vigor.

The truck pulled off in a rush of high blowing dust, and the man disappeared like a mirage. Darl watched him leave, then sat back in his chair.

"Damn sonofabitch. Saying shit about your land."

Out in the field, there was no longer Horace. Just crops.

"Our land," Parnell said. "Ours."

Darl turned and smiled.

"All right. Who's next?"

4

They had quite a few men come looking for work. Talking about their land know-how and a few saying they had heard of the farm from years back, of good food and a place to make a fine living. Darl said he was pleased, and Parnell felt happy though a bit tired of sitting.

Late in the afternoon, as they were going in for some food, a man came up the road on foot. He came and sat in the chair facing the two men. He took off his broad-brimmed straw hat, like he was in a church, doing it slowly and with grace. He wore coveralls, a white tank top and boots. He was not a young man, but tall and well-built and looked as if he could haul things.

"Do you mind if I smoke?" he asked. "It's a habit I can't quit."

"Sure," Parnell said, trying but not able to sit up a bit in the sinking chair.

Parnell had spoken up more and more as the day drew on.

"My name is Enoch," he said.

Darl laughed out loud.

"What the hell kinda name is that?" he said.

"My mother was the religious type."

"Fair enough," Darl said.

Enoch lit a cigarette, taking in the smoke with visible enjoyment.

"Well," Darl began.

"Do you mind if I tell you the truth. Might save you time," Enoch said.

Darl smiled. He seemed to like that. He glanced at Parnell. Parnell nodded, then glanced past Enoch, seeing again, the vision of Horace, which he'd seen on and off through the day and taken as a fact. Horace was kneeling. Something he had not done before.

"I am looking to settle down," Enoch said. "I have worked tobacco farms, and some others, all my life. I know land. It has not been an easy life by any means. But it's mine."

He drew regularly on the cigarette, talking in short bursts like he was savoring the smoke between the words and phrases.

"I know how to run a farm. I can tell you what to buy, how many men to hire. I can do my best to make it work for you. But I want to settle here. I see you have a barn. I can live there. I'd like to take meals with you. I'd like to stay during off season. You might say this would be my last stop."

Darl nodded his head.

"I see," Darl said. "You know what you want. That's good in a man."

"I'm alone. I do not have kin. I'm dependable. But like I said, I want to settle. I've moved around all of my life. I'm done. I figure you won't start seeding until February, but I'd like to start now. Help you get things in order."

He pulled out a new cigarette and lit it with the end of the dying one. Horace was still kneeling in the field. Parnell did not know what to make of it. But he liked what the man said. He had never had a family either. He understood that loneliness.

Willy was dead when he came into his life.

"Would you like to look at the barn?" Parnell said. "Darl can show you."

Darl stood.

"Yes, come on, let's take a look."

The two men went off and Parnell set into the job of getting himself up and out of the chair. He rolled to one side and used the side of the chair to press up. It took all his strength, as the chair was low, and it took several tries, but he got to standing. He was glad he had made it up before the men came back out. He watched them walking toward him and he had a very good feeling. He saw Horace. The man had his hands raised up over his head, looking up at the sky, and Parnell took that as a good sign. *This is another thing that is happening to me,* he thought. *And this is a good thing. Not like the bones. This is simply a good thing.*

From: The Step-by-Step Guide to Growing Tobacco, Independently Published

Germination: The tobacco seeds will germinate in 7-14 days, depending on the temperature and moisture levels in the seedbed.

5

It was Christmas. Parnell wore a coat made of two coats, two large shearling remnants from a woman who sold such things in town. It had been sliced down the center like a kill and sewn to make a large enough piece for his girth. He stood behind the house looking out at their fields.

There was a constant blow of cold snow. It had been two days since the blizzard's start. It snowed on and off, so the drifts were not enormous. The field stretched cotton pale and calm, with a sheen that sparkled with the sun, between swags of clouds. But the lightness of it never disappeared. Because the snow was so bright. *It holds its light even as the clouds pass back and forth,* he thought.

Parnell liked the snow, and now with a proper coat (something not part of his previous life story, never having outerwear that fit) he could linger, watching. The snowflakes, coming in bursts and long slow ascensions from so far above, were a wonder to behold.

He went back toward the house.

Darl was baking a ham. He had revealed a talent for cooking, beyond what might be done at the Sonic. There would be biscuits, cornbread, squash, green beans, fried okra and a pie. Enoch was setting the table. Enoch had also cut down and haphazardly decorated a small tree. There was a fire (Enoch again).

Enoch had moved into the house after a week in the barn. There was room, and they all agreed it made sense. As time passed, Enoch revealed more and more knowledge of farming, and how this could actually work. There was equipment to buy, very particular steps to planting tobacco and also sweet potatoes, which was a smart side harvest. There was not enough money, yet. But they were looking at a loan. Walking back slowly toward the front of the house, Parnell thought *Enoch is almost like our father.* It was a private thought, so he could think it. If he said it aloud, Darl would surely laugh at him or say something wise-cracking.

Parnell had not known his father. Or his mother. Only the institutions. He had never found anyone that felt like a father or a brother or sister. He only saw them in the films that had made up the fabric of his life. While bits of those many, many films for years gave him comfort and decorated a landscape of what he gladly mistook as part of his real life, he could never take it so far as to believe, *That person could be my kin, that man could be a father to me.* There was one gothic horror film where a young woman (who later turned out to be a young man, but that was a plot twist) believed her dolls were her siblings and were real. But that was just not right. Parnell knew.

He paused and turned back to the glistening white field. He no longer sought an answer to all that was happening in life through a remembered film. That was gone.

He drifted in his own small mind these days, like the snow blowing. A dance. He happily drifted.

He looked once more and scanned the field for life. He looked for Horace. But that also had gone. If he'd ever really been. He had surely been in Parnell's dream that one night, that was a fact. He had helped him find his way. But he no longer saw him. And Parnell now had a lot to do.

Inside the house, assaulted by the warmth after the harsh cold, he stomped his boots and shook out his large coat and hung it on the double hook Darl had hung by the door.

He heard Darl singing in the kitchen. He went to the living room where Enoch had moved the kitchen table. Enoch stood at one end of the table staring at a stack of plates and silverware. He was lit by the nearby fire, and everything in the room glowed and it was warm. Enoch kept staring at the stack of plates.

"What's wrong?" Parnell said.

Enoch looked up.

"Oh, it's nothing really. It's just, I've never set a table," he said. "You must think I'm crazy."

Parnell stepped in and smiled. While he had set a table, there was something altogether foreign and strange about this meal with these two men in this house on Christmas. He understood his friend's sense of discovery.

"I don't think there's a wrong way," Parnell said.

Enoch looked at Parnell, then at the plates. Then he laughed softly.

"Yes," he said.

He began to put the plates and cutlery on the table. Darl joined them.

"What I think we should do is fill up our plates in the kitchen and bring them back," he said.

"Oh," Enoch said, visibly stricken, but as he reached to pick the plates back up Darl stopped him and said, "No. Forget what I said. I'll bring the food in here."

"Is it ready?" Parnell said.

"All but the pie. They're kinda tricky. But yes, it's done and we got a feast. Go on, sit."

Enoch sat looking uneasily at the table he'd set. Parnell thought, *He can run a farm but not set a table*, and something about that comforted him.

The small, somewhat decrepit-looking tree stood in the corner. It had no lights, but the fire threw light and shadows and that gave it life.

He could hear Darl clattering about in the kitchen. Darl came out with big plates loaded with food. He brought glasses and a bottle of whiskey. He sat. Parnell looked at the plates and the two men and the fire and the tree and he had a feeling they expected him to say something, and he thought of the preacher, their friend, who was not there. He was likely doing something religious.

"This is fine," Parnell said.

Then he began to reach for the ham. Darl poured whiskey.

It was magnificent, all of it.

6

Enoch had loaded the fireplace with logs, some large and squared off, some limbs gnarled and tangled-looking. It roared. They ate Darl's pumpkin pie, which was remarkably good. After the first bite, Parnell realized he could eat the whole pie if they let him. He wished Darl had made a few more. He had expected the pie and most of the food to be good, but it was better than that. Maybe Darl had learned some secrets working at the Sonic after all.

There was another roaring sound, this from the distance, and the three men stopped eating, listening. Parnell recalled the dust devil, the ripping sound of wind that one morning, and also that sound of rain that finished the drought and the joy there. And, for some reason, he thought of Horace's voice, when he'd spoken to him in that first dream. The roar had a squeal, and it drew closer. It was a car approaching the house. Parnell continued to eat his pie, eyeing a second piece. The car stopped. Then, a knock at the door. Parnell finished his pie, then got up.

"Not expecting anyone," he said, making his way slowly to the door.

He opened it. A tall, thin man in a full-length brown fur coat and large fur hat stood staring at him. It took a moment, but he realized it was Mr. Diggs, the lawyer who had come by the day he'd arrived. He looked past the man, through the waves of snow, and he spied the blue Buick. The tires were wrapped with chains, to plow through the snow. That was all the noise.

"Come in," Parnell said, not knowing what else to do as it was Christmas and it was cold.

Mr. Diggs came in, shaking off snow, moving into the house without being asked. He went toward the main room, the two men and the fire, as if he were expected. Parnell followed, irritated but not yet afraid. He did not like the man, he hadn't the day he met him, but he did not seem threatening. Parnell went back to the table and sat. He eyed the pie again. There were several pieces left and nobody seemed to be reaching for it.

"Merry Christmas, Gentlemen," Mr. Diggs said, from the fireplace. "I've brought good tidings as they say."

Darl and Enoch looked to Parnell.

"He's a lawyer," Parnell said. "From town."

Mr. Diggs moved toward the table.

"I'll get a chair," Darl said.

He brought it in along with a glass, pouring whiskey for the man without asking.

Mr. Diggs sat, smiling.

"No, not from town. I couldn't live here. Too small. I don't know how you all do it. I'd lose my mind in a minute."

He drank down the whiskey, still smiling. Parnell wondered how anyone could smile like that for so long, then he lifted his plate and Darl cut him another piece of pie.

Parnell looked over at Mr. Diggs and thought he looked like a bear wrapped up in all that fur. He wanted to ask him why he was there, but he gave him a minute.

"Well, word is you are making a go of this farm after all,"

Mr. Diggs said. "I gotta admit I was surprised."

Darl stood, reached over, refilled the man's glass with whiskey. Mr. Diggs looked at Parnell.

"I didn't think you had it in you, sir," he said, pausing as if he'd forgotten what to say next. "I've got something for you."

He reached into the cavern of that huge coat and pulled out a white envelope and laid it on the table in front of Parnell.

"That's for you, from your Uncle Willy," Diggs said.

Parnell looked up from his pie and for a moment wondered if Willy or Horace were listening, if they had become visible in the room.

"Your uncle was an odd bird," Mr. Diggs said. "He had a good bit of money, 1.5 million to be exact."

Darl hopped up.

"You ain't shitting!" Darl said.

Parnell set down his fork, shocked and speechless.

"Which is why he hired me. It's sitting in a bank. The thing is…"

He paused, looking at Parnell.

"He set a stipulation. If after a year, you made a decision to make a go at this farm, the money was yours. If you did not, if you sold this farm or left, it was not. It went to the church."

Mr. Diggs downed his whiskey and stood up.

"I figured Christmas was good a day as any to let you know. So, well, Merry Christmas. In these parts they would say you are a rich man."

"Oh, holy fuck!" Darl said, clapping his hands.

Parnell watched Diggs, as if he would evaporate, as if he would turn into Horace and tell him this was a dream and not real. Darl lifted his arms in the air, then rushed to Parnell's side and slapped him on the back.

"Hell, man!" Darl said.

The physical touch sent a shock wave through Parnell and he began to breathe heavily, then to laugh, and Enoch stood up shaking his head and smiling.

"Well, I'll be damned." Enoch said.

"I'll be back tomorrow with the paperwork and all that," Diggs said. "But I figured I'd let you know since it's Christmas."

He stood up. Parnell was struggling to stand, still taking in the news.

"Don't bother," Diggs said. "I'll see myself out."

Parnell watched him go, and despite an urge to go out to the field, to see if Willy were there, to thank him somehow, he stood up fully and turned to Darl.

They stared at one another, both grinning, Enoch watching, and Parnell felt a great joy that he did not know how to express.

Darl reached out, took his hands and squeezed them, then released them and threw his hands up in the air and began to dance. He moved around the table in a chaotic jig, clapping his hands, slapping his knees and singing aloud, laughing and singing, and Enoch laughed along, and Parnell did something he had never done. He began to sway. With much effort, he lifted his arms as high as he could, and he moved, one foot at a time, lifting up and down, stomping in an illiterate sort of dance, lifting again, stomping again and moving with his best vigor, moving around the table in the path that Darl had sent in motion.

EPILOGUE: EARTH

There's a lightness down here, under the earth.
And a light, which might seem crazy, being that it is dark and dank and, well, earth. But then having done so much with this very same earth, feeling connected to it, depending on it, makes it feel like home.

And, for me, the lightness is a real revelation.

I'd had those visions of myself traveling across these fields. Dreamlike, yes, but a lightness I'd never experienced. That was back way before the day in July when the lightning struck, but I'll get to that.

The thing is, maybe the visions were a premonition, maybe that was Willy's master plan all along. I don't know.

I think I will know at some point, but not yet. I don't worry here, another lightness, a new part of it for me. There is a constant calm in this earth.

And we can rise. At night for some reason. Sometimes I see things. I see clearly. That is the best of the light. The seeing.

The first time was the day they dug the grave. They had to dig a real large pit. I'm not sure how they decided to bury me in our land. But the preacher was there and Enoch. And Darl was huffing and puffing and cussing, and I saw his anger and sadness and that filled me, again, with a light.

I obviously needed a very big space for my girth. And that night, being allowed for some reason to watch, I saw Horace and Willy and a lady, I'm not sure who she was. We were all allowed to watch and that was the start.

Well, no. Not really the start.

I am sorry to keep repeating myself, but there's more light to be had here. And I believe it is fine for me to go on about lightness, as my life had a good deal of heaviness. I'm not being clever. Beyond my mortal self, that affliction of size, I had a lot of grief. Not so much light.

So, the farm.

Darl, Enoch and I and all that money I got. We made quite a success of it. Five full years before the drought hit. We three, and the men we hired, it grew, not just the crops. The place. We called it P&D Farms. It grew into a sort of joyfulness, like the times before the dark patch Willy went through, back when the crops were strong and the men were happy and things were good.

Even the drought. It came. But we'd been through one before. We had faith.

Darl would go out every day and stare up at the sky, and he set into reading the farmer's almanac and even a book of rain spells. But the day it broke, the day the rain swept in, first with a smell that only rain can bring and then a feeling of something breaking free and being young and ripe and unbroken. It had been the same length of time to the day of the last drought. And I remember Darl being so happy that last time, and I thought, *I'm going to go out like he did, I'm going to feel the rain.* And I did.

And the lightning struck me. I was, let's face it, a large target.

So, now, back at the grave and Darl cussing and digging such a large hole. He even cussed at me, which made me happy somehow. "Damn it, Parnell!" he said, digging. Because he was digging. He was doing it to lay me to rest.

I do not believe I will see things this way for too much longer. I believe something is set to change. But there was something I saw which feels like it all makes sense, so this part I will tell you.

You see, sometimes I am in the earth and there is light in the dark and there are smells and voices and that is all. And sometimes I am out, alone or with others, like at my own burial, and I see.

A month after they buried me, I was out. There is no pause or moment in being out. It just is. It was late, soft black dark that too feels lit from so many bold country stars. Darl was alone in a lawn chair behind the house, looking out at the fields. Looking at my burying spot.

I cannot move on my own, in this state, which is a wonder of lightness for me, being like air. I can be brought though. By what I don't know. I was brought closer to him very slowly. Like a camera inching forward, taking a very long slow time to move closer and closer to the character in the scene.

Darl was very still, which was not like him, and he was not even smoking. As he came closer, which was me getting closer, but it felt the other way, his lips seemed to be moving. He was saying something. And closer, then closer it came, a little then more, until finally hovering close enough for a film where lovers' lips might touch but this is not that film there was a repeating and a pain on his face in each of those two words repeating and a longing that only grief can bring in those two words and I heard them just those two words and I was lit through and through filled fuller than any idea of what being full could be and I knew then why it was worth it, all of it, every moment that repeating of those two words very slowly filled so full so full because they were just for only for absolutely for me:

Come back.

www.ingramcontent.com/pod-product-compliance
Lightning Source LLC
Chambersburg PA
CBHW021153260326
41798CB00029B/379